QUESTIO

"Winning would n
and, of course, to m
for the money—though that would be great.
But to be the best at something."

"I think I know what you mean," I said.
But for me, "The Brain Game" was a fun
contest. For him, it was all-important. I knew,
observing the determination on his face, that
he couldn't let victory slip away from him as
easily as I could.

"Let's walk," Dave suggested. We strolled
around the lake leisurely. I wished this moment would last forever, that we could forget
"The Brain Game" and just be happy.

Suddenly Dave took both my hands in his
and grasped them firmly, staring into my
eyes. His gaze seemed to search mine so intently that I shivered in response. "Good
night, and good luck tomorrow," he whispered, his lips brushing mine one last time
before we parted.

Questions of Love

Rosemary Vernon

BANTAM BOOKS
TORONTO · NEW YORK · LONDON · SYDNEY · AUCKLAND

RL 5, IL age 11 and up

QUESTIONS OF LOVE

A Bantam Book / May 1985

*Sweet Dreams and its associated logo are registered trademarks of
Bantam Books, Inc. Registered in U.S. Patent and Trademark Office
and elsewhere.*

Cover photo by Pat Hill

ISBN 0-553-24945-2

Published simultaneously in the United States and Canada

Bantam Books are published by Bantam Books, Inc. Its trademark,
consisting of the words ''Bantam Books'' and the portrayal of
a rooster, is Registered in U.S. Patent and Trademark Office
and in other countries. Marca Registrada. Bantam Books, Inc.,
666 Fifth Avenue, New York, New York 10103.

PRINTED IN THE UNITED STATES OF AMERICA

O   0 9 8 7 6 5 4 3 2 1

*This book is dedicated,
with love,
to my uncle, Gerry Hunt.*

Special thanks to Ann Lieberman, producer of "The Knowledge Bowl" for NYT Cable TV, the Bordentown Scotties, and the Haddonfield Bulldogs for helping to make this book possible.

And for your unique insights on the competition, thank you, Laura Chmialewski, John Sullivan, and Alex Travis.

Chapter One

As the school's yellow van stopped in front of the television studio, all I could think was, *This is it, a dream come true. You, Sammi Edwards, are going to be on TV.* I could barely believe it was happening. I mean, I'm just a normal, basic sixteen-year-old girl.

Well, maybe not so basic. I mean, who really is? But at the moment, I was special because I was going to be on "The Brain Game." If you've never heard of it, it's a TV game show in which two high-school teams are pitted against each other in a contest of wits. And believe me, it's really exciting to be chosen for it.

The selection was a tough process, too. When our school, Wembley High, was selected for the show, all the honors students were given a test consisting of questions on every imaginable subject. Even after testing in the top one per-

cent, we still had to go through a grueling fina
selection.

It was my interest in current events tha
helped me get a spot on the show. Mr. Carma
linghi, our adviser, wanted to balance the team
with kids with different special interests. H
knew I could cover questions on recent history
I'm also interested in women's history.

My interest in the women's movement was an
outgrowth of my belief in myself. I'm opinion
ated and have always been outspoken. I even
dress differently from most girls. I like wild fash
ions or offbeat clothes from tag sales. Fo
instance, that day I was wearing a red minidres
with low-heeled, ankle-length, red canvas boot
and a scarf that matched my shoulder-length
auburn hair. I wore large loopy earrings and a
string of aqua-colored glass beads that high
lighted my blue-green eyes. Even without m
flamboyant clothes, I stand out because I'm s
tall.

I glanced at my four teammates, Alan Whitlaw
Jessie Klein, Shelley Norman, and my bes
friend, Melody Williams. They all looked about a
nervous as I felt. Even Mr. Carmalinghi seemed a
little flustered. My brain, which I was counting
on to exhibit its true worth, was fast deterior
ating into a useless mass of frightened gray mat
ter.

But my jelly brain would have to do. I'd been

waiting for this day for months, ever since we'd been notified in early spring that we'd be the contestants on a July run of "The Brain Game." I'd even picked out the car I would put a down payment on if I won, a cute little red Toyota.

It wasn't until Mr. Carmalinghi told the team we'd better get going that we realized we'd all been sitting in the van staring at the TV studio. I was a little disappointed when I first saw the long, squat, concrete-block building of CAT Cable TV. It looked forbidding and unfriendly, like a large think tank. Of course, from watching so many programs, we knew the "Brain Game" set was colorful and pleasant. But it sure didn't seem that way from the outside.

"Are you ready for this?" Melody whispered to me as we climbed out of the van.

"No!" I whispered back, and we both giggled.

"This building looks like a tomb," commented Alan Whitlaw as he straightened his tie. He's the most talented science student in our school.

"Or a place where they do illegal brain experiments," said Shelley Norman. She's a tall, heavyset girl with an engaging smile and a booming laugh. She also happens to know almost anything about art, music, theater, and dance.

Jessie Klein, who's into philosophy and mythology, said, "Well, here's one small step for mankind."

"And womankind," Melody corrected him with a smile at me. She knew I had been thinking exactly the same thing.

Mel and I have been friends since the third grade, which is why we know how the other thinks. When we first met, Mel had just moved to town and couldn't copy the spelling words off the board before the teacher erased them. But she was so shy, she didn't say a word. So big-mouthed me asked the teacher if she could please slow down so *we* could copy all the words. Melody flashed me a huge smile, and we've been inseparable ever since.

Now, Melody's a writer, and she's read just about every novel and poem in the whole world. Well, that's an exaggeration, but not by much. She also takes Spanish, which Mr. Carmalinghi thought might help on the game. She's gorgeous, with honey blond hair and big violet eyes.

"Why don't you all stop gawking and make a few strides over this way," Mr. Carmalinghi said, herding us toward the building. He grinned at me as I passed. "I see you're dressed for success today, Sammi," he commented.

"My good-luck dress," I said.

"Nice to have someone with style on the team," my adviser continued. "An individualist."

Just then we heard a car and all watched a Volvo station wagon come to a stop. Our competitors from Rushmore High climbed out of the

4

ar. "The enemy has arrived," Jessie Klein murmured.

Melody pointed to a slim black girl with an Afro haircut. "That's Ophelia Long, last year's county spelling champ," she said. Rushmore is another high school in our town, Springfield, so we know a lot of the kids who go there.

"There's Desiree Whitney," Alan said as a short, blond girl glanced our way. "She was in a math contest I entered in September. She's a real computer whiz."

"Hey, I didn't know Ron Bedford would be here," said Jessie. "He used to date my sister. He's really into anthropology. A real brain."

"Teddy Cummings will probably be your competition for current events questions, Sammi," said Shelley. "But I can't imagine him concentrating hard enough to be a threat."

Just then Melody nudged me in the ribs. She didn't need to. I was already staring at the tall, chestnut-haired boy with light gray eyes who had just stepped out of the driver's side of another car. His nose was straight and narrow, and his arched eyebrows gave him a friendly, surprised expression. "That's Dave Handlin," said Shelley. "He's their history buff, and he's really good."

"He's sensational looking," Melody said—a more basic description than Shelley's.

I turned to Melody to agree, but she'd already

started to follow the others to the building
When I glanced back, Dave was looking right a
me. He smiled, then walked casually my way.
didn't know what to do, so I just said hi.

He nodded, still grinning, and said, "Hi. Goo
luck."

"You, too," I told him. He walked over to joi
his team, and I ran to catch up with mine at th
front entrance.

It was a mild enough conversation. Bu
already I knew there was nothing mild about m
interest in David Handlin. Nothing mild at all.

Chapter Two

Melody yanked open the double glass doors to the studio, and we stepped inside. "Shelley says Dave won an all-state history contest last year," she told me. "He's definitely someone to keep an eye on."

"That's for sure," I remarked, but I meant it in a different way.

I had a feeling about Dave, a feeling I hadn't had about anyone since Derek and I had broken up six months before when I won the Springfield Trivia Contest. Our breakup boiled down to the fact that Derek was jealous of my becoming momentarily famous. Someone from the *Sentinel*, our local paper, took my picture and wrote one short article about me. That's what I mean by "momentarily famous." People forget who you are almost instantly, which is fine with me. I didn't lose my head over the whole thing. But

Derek did. I pleaded with him to give our rela
tionship one more try, but he insisted on break
ing up. He said we didn't have anything in com
mon anymore.

Well, maybe we never really had anything in
common to begin with, but that didn't matter a
the time. The breakup really hurt because I wa
crazy about him. Anyway, after Derek I swore of
guys for a while. Then, gradually, I began datin
again, but no one special. I figured I'd neve
meet anyone I could really care for again. Yet on
look at David Handlin showed me that I *coul*
get interested in someone again.

By the time our team found the way to th
"Brain Game" conference room, I wasn't sure i
the butterflies in my stomach were because of th
upcoming game or Dave's smile. Probably a bit o
both.

But once we were settled in the conferenc
room, excitement for the game took over, and
pushed Dave out of my mind for the moment.
did sneak an occasional glance at him, but
knew I had to concentrate. The program'
coproducer, Lucinda Brown, welcomed us to th
show and told us to make ourselves comfortabl
in the little room. Then she introduced us to th
judge, Bill Krupp, who compiled all the ques
tions and checked our answers.

It was then that Ty Carlin came into the room
He's the show's host, so of course we all recog

nized him. We clapped as he entered, and he smiled a little self-consciously. His grin was warm, and he immediately made me feel at home.

"Hi, everybody," he said, giving a shake of his curly blond hair. He sat down in a chair nearby.

"OK," Lucinda continued. "I'm sure you all know the rules, so we'll skip those. There are a few things I need to remind you of before you go on television. One, please remember to wait for Ty to nod to you before answering a question. Two, arguments about rulings must wait until after the show. Mikes will be on at all times. Three, at the end of the show, please don't get up and walk off the stage until we say it's OK. The cameras may still be on you. But most important, have fun. Remember, you're here to have a good time." A few groans erupted from the group.

Lucinda asked us to introduce ourselves, which we did quickly. I watched Ty's face as we spoke, and he seemed to be memorizing our names.

"So, now that I know who you are," Ty said, pushing himself out of his chair, "I have a few tips for each of you on how to make the show exciting. Be sure you speak up. It's a must, especially since our judge, Mr. Krupp, sits a considerable distance from you. Audiences love to hear byplay between the two teams, but they don't want to hear any poor sportsmanship. At the opening, introduce yourself in this way—full name, what grade you're in, where you're from. If you have any idea what you want to do with your life, tell us, then tell us about any activities, hobbies, et cetera. If you feel comfortable, poke a little fun at yourself and one another."

Ophelia Long giggled. "That shouldn't be too hard," she quipped, and everyone laughed.

"Don't hesitate to guess—it can't cost you anything," Ty said. "Now, I know you're anxious and nervous, but have fun, anyway. Good luck, and I'll see you in the studio!"

We all rose, and everyone talked animatedly as we filed into the studio behind the adults. Dave strode ahead of me, looking cool and confident. *Maybe he's one of those types who never gets ruffled*, I speculated.

The studio itself was very small, painted bright blue. There was a big closed-circuit TV in one corner, facing the bleachers where the audience would sit. Three cameras were set up, all pointing to the stage. There was a high platform on either side of the stage, with a long desk where each team would sit. Behind each desk were a lighted scoreboard and the "Brain Game" logo. All of our names were displayed prominently on name boards in front of our seats. As one of us hit a buzzer, his or her name would light up. We all were given pads and pencils for figuring.

We filed in and took our seats, waiting nervously as the audience came in. I scanned the crowd until I found my family. My dad had taken the afternoon off from work.

Mom looked trim and regal in her peach linen dress. She has the same russet-colored hair as I do, and she's tall like me, too. My sister, Katie, looks more like my dad. They both have dark hair and brown eyes. Dad is imposing because he's very tall and handsome. Katie, who's a year younger than I am, had on her favorite pinstriped shirtwaist dress, her usual conservative attire. We're very different. My parents seem to approve of her style more than mine.

Ty walked to the front of the stage and addressed the audience. "You may applaud when your team scores, but don't overdo it, or we'll never finish the contest. No booing, whistling, or other distracting sounds. Now, contestants, try your buzzers." There was a bumblebee concerto as everyone pressed the buttons. "Keep your fingers on the buzzers at all times. You won't need pencils and paper unless I tell you. So let's have a great show!" Everyone applauded until Ty held his hand up for silence. "I'm going to ask the teams a few practice questions. Are you ready?"

There was a chorus of groans and mumbled

yeses. We hunched over our desks, fingers poised over our buzzers.

"What was the treaty that ended the Spanish-American War?" Ty asked.

David hit his buzzer. "Treaty of Paris."

"Correct. Name two territories acquired by the U.S. as a result of that treaty?"

Jessie hit his buzzer. "Guam and Cuba."

"I'm sorry, Cuba is not correct. It's Guam, Puerto Rico, and the Phillipines."

"What creatures inhabited the Shires?"

Melody buzzed. "Hobbits," she said.

"Correct answer. What Lewis Carroll character sings, 'Twinkle, twinkle, little bat'?"

Ophelia pressed her buzzer. "The Mad Hatter."

"Correct answer." Ty riffled through his blue cards, which held all the questions for our game. "OK, end of practice questions, it's getting close to show time, folks. Countdown . . ."

On the closed-circuit TV, the lively Vivaldi music began, and then the taped introduction: "CAT cable TV presents the summer season of 'The Brain Game,' an innovative approach to academic competition, where competitors vie for a school prize of five thousand dollars and an individual prize of five thousand dollars. And here is Ty Carlin, host of 'The Brain Game'!"

"Welcome, folks," Ty said, grinning. "As you may know, this is a very special contest on 'The

Brain Game.' This month we have teams from schools in our own hometown, Springfield. And I'm sure all of Springfield is watching. Who will win? In the next half hour, we'll come close to finding out. And now, welcome the Wembley Giants and the Rushmore Royals!"

The audience exploded with applause. After a moment Lucinda, standing in front, held up a card signaling everyone to be quiet.

"Our judge tonight is Bill Krupp, director of library services at Winthrop College, and here's a brief rundown on our rules," Ty continued rapidly. "Each question is worth ten points. There is no penalty for wrong answers, but the other team does get a chance to correct the mistake and win the points. At the end of the game we tally up the number of questions each player has answered, and the player on each team with the least points is eliminated from the next game. This process continues for four games, until the final battle in which one player from each team competes for the five-thousand-dollar prize. But even the losing player can be a winner, if his or her school has won more games and snags the five-thousand-dollar school prize." Ty smiled at all the contestants, then went on. "On my left, folks, I have the Wembley Giants. Team, would you tell us a little bit about yourselves?"

At that moment my heart jumped, and I was sure my words would come out in squeaks. I

13

took a deep breath. I wanted my first televised sentence to be perfect. Of course, I did fine. Wembley's introductions all went well, and the audience laughed when Alan Whitlaw said his career goal was to wear a lab coat for the rest of his life. Rushmore's introductions went equally smoothly.

Then Ty said the magic words, "Is everyone ready to go? OK, let's get on with the contest!" And before I had time even to bite a fingernail, I was in the middle of my first "Brain Game." Ty shuffled the pack of blue question cards, took the top one, and read: "What North American colony became a haven for persecuted Catholics?"

A buzzer sounded loudly, and at first I wasn't even sure who had pressed it. It was Dave—of course. He'd probably know all the history answers. "Maryland," he pronounced.

"Correct answer. Ten points for Rushmore," Ty said, and the scoreboard lit up. "Name the nineteenth-century monk whose scientific research laid the foundation for modern genetics."

Jessie buzzed. "Gregor Mendel."

"That is correct. Ten points for Wembley, bringing the two teams to a tie." Ty leafed through his cards. "Two Italians sailed from Spain and are remembered in many Western place names. Who are they?"

"Christopher Columbus and Amerigo Vespucci," replied Ophelia.

"Correct! Rushmore now has twenty points to Wembley's ten. Slavery was outlawed in the colony—"

Melody interrupted the question with her buzzer. I held my breath, hoping she was right about the end of Ty's sentence.

"Georgia," she replied.

"Correct! The question: 'Slavery was outlawed in the colony that was founded by James Oglethorpe. Which colony?' Georgia is the correct answer. Each team has twenty points. OK, name the author who offered, 'nothing more than simple facts, plain arguments and common sense' in his pamphlet published in 1776."

"Thomas Paine," replied Dave.

"Ten more points for Rushmore!" cried Ty. "For ten points each, name the two scientists who discovered the structure of the molecule that contains hereditary information."

Ron Bedford answered: "James Watson and Crippen."

"Ten points for the first answer. Watson is correct. But the second one is not. Wembley?"

Alan buzzed for that one. "Francis Crick."

"That is correct! What form of pollution is killing lake life throughout the northeastern United States and Europe?"

I went for my buzzer, but Teddy Cummings got to his first. "Acid rain," he said.

"That's right. The score is fifty to thirty, Rushmore leading, as we take this break. Stay tuned for the next part of 'The Brain Game' after this factual message about our two competing schools."

Darn, I thought, *I should have gotten that answer.* If I was going to get anywhere in this game, I'd have to move a little faster.

Ty relaxed while the closed-circuit television set showed a taped message outlining some of the activities and projects of both high schools. It was interesting to see what professionals could do with a camera. I loved the way they made our school sound like some expensive resort to visit. Of course, it never felt that way when you had to get up every morning and go.

As the film rolled, I scanned the two teams, looking enviously at the kids who had already answered questions. I hated to admit it, but I was getting a little worried. Not about Rushmore's lead. That was only twenty points, and I knew we could make up the points with two right answers. Not even about the tough competition Rushmore was giving us, because I knew we were giving them a good fight, too.

The thing was, I hadn't answered a single question yet. What if I didn't answer any and I was the first person to be dropped from the show? It was as if I weren't really concentrating. *Think, Sammi,* I told myself as Ty walked back to the center of the stage to begin the show again. *Put your mind into this.*

"Welcome to the second round of 'The Brain Game'!" Ty said heartily. "Rules are exactly the same. Contestants, keep those fingers on the buzzers at all times. Here we go! What famous Parisian street is named for the Elysian fields?"

I buzzed my buzzer. "Champs Élysées," I replied, struggling awkwardly with the accent. I'd never taken any French.

"Right answer, but I'm sorry to tell you, Sammi, your pronunciation is terrible."

Everyone laughed, but I felt an immense sense of relief at finally getting an answer. I guess I had been a little tongue-tied at first, but I knew it would be easier now that I'd gotten my first question out of the way.

Ty went on. "Country singer Crystal Gayle has an older sister whose life was the basis for a recent movie. Name that sister."

I pressed my buzzer. "Loretta Lynn." *Maybe I'm on a roll*, I thought happily to myself.

"Our teams are tied at fifty points," said Ty. "What does it mean when a substance is said to be 'carcinogenic'?"

Alan hit his buzzer. "It causes cancer."

"Sixty points for Wembley, fifty for Rushmore." I reflected briefly on how quickly a lead could be turned around in this game. Ty continued, "Now, tell us, what is the branch of medicine that deals with the study of tumors?"

Ron replied, "Oncology."

"Correct answer, adding ten points to Rushmore for a sixty-point tie. What was the pony's name in John Steinbeck's story, 'The Red Pony'?"

"Gabilan," replied Melody.

"Correct answer. Name the youngest president of the United States."

I answered, "John F. Kennedy."

"That is correct, Wembley Giants, and you now have eighty points to Rushmore's sixty. Name the author of the famous poem about making choices, 'The Road Not Taken.' "

Melody and Ophelia pressed their buzzers almost at the same time, but Melody got to hers first. "Robert Frost," she replied.

"That's right," Ty said. His manner was more enthusiastic as the game went on. Ty picked up another blue card. "Isadora Duncan was a pioneer of what field?"

Shelley buzzed. "Modern dance," she said.

"Good. That's one hundred to sixty, Wembley leading."

The Wembley cheering section went wild, and Lucinda had to tell them to quiet down. "This is the end of the second round, audience," he said.

"We'll return to our exciting game after this message."

I looked at the other team and found a pair of light gray eyes gazing at me. I shivered, smiled at Dave, then dropped my gaze to my blank memo pad. The show began once more, and I shook Dave's image from my thoughts.

"What famous inventor helped found the Library Company of Philadelphia?" Ty asked.

Dave hit his buzzer. "Ben Franklin."

"Correct. Rushmore has seventy points to Wembley's one hundred. Listen carefully. What position did Robert Kennedy hold in President John F. Kennedy's cabinet?"

Ophelia answered promptly. "Attorney general," she said.

"Correct answer, giving Rushmore eighty points to Wembley's one hundred. What is the function of a catalyst?"

Alan answered this time. "To speed up or start a chemical reaction."

"Another ten points for Wembley, bringing that team's total up to one hundred and ten points. Next question. What set of tales was written by Geoffrey Chaucer?"

Melody hit her buzzer. "*The Canterbury Tales*," she replied. A whoop erupted from the Wembley section.

"Wembley now has a total of one hundred twenty points to Rushmore's eighty. The equinox occurs in March and September. What is equal during the equinox?"

"The days and nights are equal," Ophelia said.

"That's right. Ninety points for Rushmore, one hundred twenty points for Wembley. OK, then what is the position of the sun at the time of the equinox?"

Jessie Klein hit his buzzer. "The center of the sun is right over the earth's equator."

"Correct answer for Wembley, bringing that team's score up to one hundred thirty points. What language is the official language in every South American country except for one?"

Desiree hit her buzzer. "Spanish."

"Yes! It's one hundred thirty to one hundred. For the final question of today's game, name the country and the language it speaks."

Desiree went for it again. "Portuguese is spoken in Brazil!" She said the answer excitedly, and I could tell she was glad she'd gotten to answer a few questions before the end.

"You've got it. The finishing score for tonight is Wembley, one hundred thirty points, Rushmore, one hundred ten. Wembley is our winner!" The audience went wild. Finally they quieted down, and Ty closed the show. "It was an exciting and close match. Good game, we really appreciate your trying so hard, and we'll see these two teams battle it out next week at this same time. Until then, good night!"

The Vivaldi concerto began again, a lilting rhythm. We had to sit quietly until Ty said we could leave our seats, and believe me, that was hard. I wanted to bounce out of my chair and go find my parents and friends.

When it was all over, my parents came over, and Mom gave me a huge hug. "Wonderful game, Sammi. You were great!" she said. She accidentally knocked off one of my loopy earrings in the process of hugging me, and it went flying. Before I even had a chance to look for it, my father said, "Sammi, I can't believe you wore those dreadful earrings." He glared disapprovingly at me.

"Oh, Dad, can't you at least say something nice for a change?" Katie asked in my behalf. It was so typical of him to make remarks like that. Mom always assured me he didn't mean to be unkind, but it hurt anyway. Mom said he just felt more comfortable with ultraconservatism. But I wished he'd accept me the way I was.

Suddenly I felt a tap on my shoulder. I turned around to find Dave holding my earring up to the light. "Dropped something?" he asked.

"Oh, uh, yes, thank you." I took it from him.

"It's an unusual earring," he commented.

My father sighed. "Yes, it is. I think Sammi lifted them from the tribal artifacts section of the county museum."

Dave laughed, and I knew I was blushing.

21

Quickly I introduced him to my family, wishing they would disappear into thin air so I didn't have to deal with them. Sometimes my father could be so embarrassing!

"The teams and their friends are meeting at Cleo's afterward. Are you going, Sammi?" Dave asked me.

I liked how he said my name in that deep, resonant voice of his. "Sounds like fun." I looked at my parents, willing them to say it was OK.

"What a good idea," Dad said jovially, and I could've kissed him. Maybe he was trying to redeem himself for his earlier comments. Maybe Mom was pinching him. Who knows?

We all walked outside, and as we were walking toward the parking lot, Melody caught up with me.

"I thought I lost you, Sam," she said. "I've got my car. My mom drove it over because she came from home and my dad came from work. Do you want to go to Cleo's?"

"Sure, I think it will be fun." I said goodbye to my parents, glad that I didn't have to depend on them for a ride. And I didn't want Dave to feel he had to drive me.

"Well, I'll see you over there, then," Dave said. He turned to walk away, then turned back again. "Sammi," he said softly. I felt the warmth of his smile touch me. "Congratulations."

"Thank you," I said, staring into those captivating light gray eyes.

It had been some day already, and I had a feeling there was still more excitement to come.

Chapter Three

Melody and I drove over to Cleo's, high on our victory. "If we do this well for the rest of the game, we'll be unbeatable," I announced, turning down the radio.

"Don't get overconfident, Sam. You know that's lethal." Melody guided her Volkswagen Rabbit into a parking space in the parking lot. "It's a good thing you're not seeing Derek anymore. Just think how mad he'd be to find out how well you did."

"Ugh. End of subject, please." It still upset me to think about my old boyfriend. "What do you think of Dave?" I asked, moving the conversation to a more pleasant topic.

"I think he's very cute, definitely smart, nice— but you've already formed your opinion of him, right?" She winked at me.

"Right. But I always have to have yours," I said and smiled as we got out of the car.

Cleo's used to be a truck stop, but was now our hangout. It's oddly decorated. There's one stained-glass window barely secured in the front door, and the tables are covered with old newspaper clippings and shellacked. So if you're on a boring date, you can always read the old news.

All the tables were taken, and Melody and I squeezed through a group of people to get to the counter, where we ordered sodas.

"I'll get that." A hand reached around me and rested on the polished wood counter. I turned around and gazed up into Dave's face. He smiled, and the lights behind him cast a halo around his head.

"It's OK, really, I've got—" I said, stumbling on my own words.

Just then Melody nudged me in the ribcage. Dave placed a five-dollar bill on the counter, and I realized that this was no time to argue about who was going to pay. "Oh, thank you," I said with a gracious smile.

"You're welcome," Dave replied, then scanned the mob. "Guess there's nowhere for us to sit, huh?"

"If you'll excuse me," Melody said, "I'm going to go pick Alan's brain for a while. See you."

"I guess we'll just have to stand here," I said,

putting my soda down and leaning against the counter.

Dave bent close to me and whispered in my ear. "What I want to know, Sammi, is this. Did you or did you not take those earrings from the tribal collection at the museum?"

I laughed. "Oh, don't believe anything my father says! He's always teasing me about the way I dress."

Dave regarded me slowly, cocking his head to one side. "Well, I like how you look. You have style." He shrugged, the beginning of a blush on his cheeks. "I never think much about what people wear. But in your case, I thought right off that you must be a real individual. You don't fit into any category."

I couldn't resist teasing him. "Well, underneath this *exotic* exterior is a preppie just waiting to get out."

"No kidding?" He laughed.

"I am in no way a preppie," I hurriedly assured him. "I just have this thing about being myself, being an individual. It drives my father crazy, of course."

By that time I was slurping the soda at the bottom of my cup. I liked the way Dave was watching me. "Want another?" he inquired.

"No, thank you. Too many sodas and I'd slosh all the way home."

"I could drive you." A hint of a smile crossed his features.

"Oh, really? Great," I said enthusiastically. "Let me tell Melody I'm leaving," I said, grabbing my bag and dashing off to find her.

Dave led me out of Cleo's and toward a Datsun sedan, speckled with rust. "I'm getting a new car, if and when I win 'The Brain Game,'" I said, getting into the car and running my finger along the frayed upholstery.

"Really?" Dave seemed interested. "Is it going to be unusual, like you?" He started the car and pulled out of the lot.

I giggled. "Blue with purple polka dots. By the way, I live on Freemont Avenue, over by Glenn Street."

"OK, I know where that is. What're you doing with yourself this summer?" he asked after a pause.

I shrugged. "Oh, just the usual. Swimming, reading, planning for our vacation. We're going to Canada this year."

"Hmmm."

"What about you?"

"I'm working—tutoring, which I enjoy. It keeps my brain from getting moldy."

I laughed. "Nothing wrong with a slightly moldy brain over summer vacation." I stopped, becoming a little more serious. "I hear you're a history buff."

27

"Yep, history's my thing. I'm going to major in it. I don't know what I'll do in the way of a career, though. I'm just going to go to college and figure it all out as I go along."

"That seems wise. I'm pretty sure what I want to do, though. I want to go into television, probably as a newscaster."

"Then you must really be excited about being on 'The Brain Game,' " Dave surmised. "First time on TV?"

"Yes, it is. I've been on radio, though, when I won last year's trivia contest."

"Oh, yeah? You won that?" He was silent for a moment. The breeze blew in through the car window, ruffling my hair. Branches formed a lacy filigree, which canopied the road leading to my house. "I think I remember seeing your picture in the paper," he said pensively.

"Yes, you might have. Oh, wait, stop. This is my driveway." I pointed up a pebbled drive to our white house, which was partially hidden from the road by a cluster of trees. "This is the place," I said, picking up my bag.

"I bet it has a history," he said as we started up the driveway.

"Yes, it does. It was built in 1790. If only the walls could talk," I said, smiling.

"Hey, Sammi, do you think we could go out this weekend? Maybe see a movie or something?" Dave stopped the car and reached for my arm. The pressure of his fingers sent ripples through me.

I was so happy that it took me a moment to respond, even though I knew right away what my answer would be. "I'd love to."

"How about tomorrow night?"

"OK."

"I'll call you about the time."

"Fine. We're in the phone book."

"Great."

I stood outside and watched Dave drive off. My hand traveled up to where he had squeezed my arm. I was so excited. And I couldn't wait to tell Melody!

"OK, what's the story?" Melody asked as I opened our front door for her. She had come straight from Cleo's because she knew I'd have news to unload.

We hurried up the stairs and down the long hallway to my room. Beyond my window was a perfect view of the New England countryside, with a brook and even a duck pond. My room's furnished in white wicker—a rocker, a bed, desk, and dresser. There are also two comfortable chairs for when friends come over. I like plants, so my windowsill is full of them, and my shelves are cluttered with books and knick-knacks that I've gathered from flea markets and yard sales.

Melody and I sat cross-legged on the floor, facing each other; she leaned forward eagerly. "OK, spill," she ordered.

"Well, we're going out Saturday night to a movie or something."

Melody clapped her hands together. "Oh, that's great. What a terrific day!" she exclaimed.

"It sure is—first 'The Brain Game,' then this. So, anyway, he tutors, and he's going to major in history in college." I leaned back against a stack of newspapers—I read one every day—and closed my eyes. "You know," I confessed, "in a way I'm kind of scared to go out with him. I mean, I haven't really dated anybody I liked in such a long time, Mel."

Melody patted my hand. "You'll do fine, Sammi. It'll all come back to you, I'm sure. Even if he *is* on the opposite team, he seems like a nice guy."

"Hey, you know, I forgot all about that!" I exclaimed. All of a sudden, I was worried. "I wonder if we should wait to date until after the game," I said thoughtfully.

"Naw, why do that?"

"What if he doesn't . . . ?" I left the thought hanging in midair.

"What if he doesn't win, and you do?" she finished for me softly.

I bent my head and nodded, recalling vividly the pain of Derek's leaving me. Derek always felt as if he didn't quite measure up, that I was too smart for him. What would happen if Dave felt the same way?

"You'll just have to take that chance," Melody said gently.

"You're right," I answered. Of course, it was too early to be thinking about that. And Dave was a different kind of boy, probably more like me, or he wouldn't have agreed to go on the show in the first place. I sighed.

"Don't look so sad," she said. "Just take things slowly with Dave."

"I'll try," I said, smiling. " 'Tis better to have loved and lost than never to have loved at all,' " I quoted. "And maybe this time I *won't* lose."

Melody's and my friendship is good for both of us: her cautiousness rubs off on me and helps me get through difficult situations, and sometimes my outgoing nature rubs off on her, helping her to be less shy and try activities she's a little afraid of—like tackling the "Brain Game" test, for instance.

Melody flipped a lock of her shiny blond hair over her shoulder. "You're an inspiration to me, Sammi," she said.

"So are you, to me. Now let's get to the paper. Do you want the classified section?"

"Sure."

We made a ritual of scanning newspapers together. Lately Melody was looking for a part-time job so she'd have extra money for clothes and because she wanted to see what it was like to work. Neither of us had to worry about money much. I had just about everything I wanted, and I could always ask my parents if I needed something. Once in a while, I baby-sat for a neighbor, but it was usually as a favor and not because I needed to make money. I put the money I earned in the bank or bought clothes or records with it. Melody's pretty much the same way.

"Here's an ad for an envelope addresser," she said. "But that sounds pretty boring."

"Yes, but it wouldn't interfere with your writing."

She used a felt pen to circle that one and another one for a waitress in a burger place.

Melody stayed for dinner that night. We had lasagne, made with spinach lasagne noodles. Mom always came up with weird dishes—you never knew exactly what you'd be served when you ate at our house. "I've never had this before," remarked Melody. "It's delicious."

"Thank you, Melody," Mom said, beaming. "You know, we haven't had the same dinner twice in six months."

"A little regularity might be in order," grumbled my father, who is a meat-and-potatoes man.

My mother looks pretty conservative on the outside, but when it comes to cooking, she's more like me—unconventional. That's why she can understand me when my father doesn't.

Now, she sighed and patted my father's hand. "Oh, Thomas, relax. You enjoy trying new things more than you'll admit. But I'll fix a nice traditional roast beef on Sunday just for you."

He shook his head. "That will be nice, Beth. But between now and then, I can be assured of every ethnic food from here to Bombay."

My sister laughed. "We already had Indian food this week," she said.

After dinner Melody and I offered to do the dishes, which made Katie very happy. "Now I can go and work on my boring geometry," she said. She was taking an advanced summer school course. "I'll do the same for you someday, Sammi."

"Write an IOU, just in case you forget," I told her.

"Such trust," she grumbled, heading off to her room.

When we finished clearing up, we played Trivial Pursuit, the game that all of us "Brain Game" contestants practiced with. The questions are very similar to the ones asked on the show, so it helped us keep in shape. Another thing we'd do for practice was to read the papers daily, although I'd done that for many years anyway. And once a week our team met with Mr. Carmalinghi to play practice games, watch old tapes of "The Brain Game," and go over current events for the upcoming show.

At around nine o'clock the phone rang. It was Dave.

"Hi," he said. "I wanted to tell you what time I'll pick you up tomorrow night." He cleared his throat. I wondered if he was as nervous phoning me as I was hearing from him.

"Oh, OK. What time?"

"How about six-thirty? The movie starts at seven-fifteen."

"Great."

"What're you up to?" he asked after a pause.

"Oh, Melody and I are playing Trivial Pursuit."

"Aha. I've been playing a lot of that myself lately."

I laughed, which I think broke the ice. "Yes, I guess we're all a little hooked, aren't we?"

"I just finished a tutoring session, myself," Dave remarked.

"Is your pupil a future 'Brain Game' entrant?"

"Could be," he said, laughing. "He's a real fan."

"You're probably a good teacher," I said.

"Thank you," he replied softly.

"So what are we going to see?" I asked.

"There's a good old romantic suspense at the Del Mar. I mean, if you're interested in it."

"I'd love to see it."

"OK, well, I'd better hang up. See you tomorrow."

I listened for the dial tone before I replaced the receiver. Melody stood next to me, grinning, waiting to hear the parts of the conversation she hadn't overheard. She placed her hands on her hips and suppressed a giggle.

"That was Dave," I announced unnecessarily.

"Yes, I could tell by the tone of your voice." She burst out giggling. "It suddenly looks like Trivial Pursuit has become far too trivial for you."

"Very funny, Mel," I retorted. But I knew she was absolutely right. My mind was no longer quite so dedicated to Trivial Pursuit as it had been five minutes before.

Chapter Four

The team met Saturday morning with Mr. Carmalinghi to quiz one another. It was just Jessie, Alan, Melody, and me, since Shelley had been dropped from the competition. Teddy Cummings was the unlucky one eliminated from Rushmore's team.

Before going out that night, I read the newspapers, took a shower, and even put on some makeup, something I don't normally do. I tried my hair three different ways before deciding to wear it down. I rejected several outfits before settling on cropped white pants, a hot pink blouse, cut short enough to reveal a slice of tanned midriff, and some pink and lime green beads and bangles.

Katie appeared in the doorway of my room. "You look like an after-dinner mint," she observed dryly.

"Gee, thanks." I stared at my reflection critically and saw what she meant. I pulled off the pink and green accessories and replaced them with gold. "How's that?"

"Much better. You want to dazzle him, not overwhelm him."

"True." I had to admit she was right, although I didn't like getting advice from my younger sister. But none of that mattered when the doorbell rang. I was just glad to look good.

Katie went to get the door. I followed quickly to find Dave talking to Mom and Dad.

"This is a great house," he said.

"Thanks," my mother replied. "Sometime we'll give you a guided tour."

"I'd love it." Dave saw me and smiled. "Hi, Sammi. You look nice."

"Thanks. So do you." He had on a gray chambray shirt and white pants. He'd combed his chestnut-colored hair straight back, making him look like a thirties movie star.

"You were terrific on 'The Brain Game,' " my father said, complimenting Dave.

"Thanks." Dave grinned at me, his gray eyes flashing. "The opposition's pretty tough, though."

"Oh, I'm sure you'll give them a run for their money," Dad said, raising an eyebrow at me. "Well, have fun. Just get my daughter home before she turns into the Great Pumpkin, that's all I ask."

"She looked like Peppermint Patty earlier, Daddy," Katie interjected.

"Oh, no," I groaned, clapping my hand over my forehead in mock despair.

"She's not doing too badly tonight." Dad surveyed me with his characteristic eagle eye.

Once we were outside Dave remarked, "I see what you mean about your father. He's not exactly crazy about anything even vaguely offbeat, is he?"

I laughed. "No, he isn't, and neither is my sister. But sometimes she helps tone me down so he doesn't find me too outrageous. He'd really like me to be like her."

"I think you should stay just the way you are," Dave said, giving me a tender smile.

"Thanks," I said shyly as we got into his car. I felt awkward. I wasn't used to receiving compliments from boys. Mostly they teased me. If I wore a new outfit on Monday morning, some boy would very likely say, "Hey, Edwards, you must've hit a good tag sale this weekend." But the compliment felt much better.

We drove along for a while in silence, and then I said, "You know, sometimes I wonder if I'm adopted."

He laughed. "I used to think about that, too,

but since there's an awfully strong family resemblance, it's doubtful."

"But a lot of the time I do feel like I'm on a different planet from my parents," I confided. "Especially my father."

"I guess everybody feels that way sometimes," he said.

There's only so long you can talk about your parents, so I asked, "Have you thought of what college you want to go to yet?"

"I'm applying to Ivy League schools. I know I'll get in and probably get a scholarship for tuition. But I hope for a bit more besides," Dave said.

I watched Dave's profile while he drove. I liked his hairline and the curve of the bone below his eye. "I'll probably pick a college on the East Coast, too," I said, "since I want to go into newscasting."

"I guess that's where the best news jobs are," he replied.

"What do you think of the people on your team?" I asked.

He turned and frowned at me. "Isn't that an off limits question? I can just hear the buzzer sounding on that one."

I laughed. "Sorry, didn't think. The main thing we have in common, we can't talk about," I noted. "What about your family? That's safe, isn't it?"

"It's not too out of the ordinary. I have three sisters, two parents, a dog, and a cat."

"What will you do with the prize money, if you win?"

"Use it for college, what else?" He grinned at me, shaking his head.

"Oh, yeah."

We rode in comfortable silence the rest of the way. Dave parked the car, then took my hand as we walked toward the theater. We were going to see a romantic adventure, which made me feel great. I mean, how many guys take you to see a romance? Usually it's something scary, or it's a Clint Eastwood movie in which good old Clint plays a drifter, mumbling an entire two sentences throughout the whole movie. I was impressed with Dave's choice.

We sat near the back of the theater. During the first half of the movie, Dave put his arm around the back of my chair and lightly stroked the top of my arm. I wanted to nestle in his shoulder, but I felt we didn't know each other well enough for that. And when the leading lady kissed her man on screen, I just stopped myself from leaning over and kissing Dave. But at that moment he removed his arm from the back of my chair and he reached down and took my hand, sending delicious ripples of excitement through me.

When the movie was over and we were back in the car, Dave asked me how I liked the movie.

"I loved it. It was so romantic," I said.

"I liked the way he came back to the woman in the end, didn't you?"

"Oh, yes. That was great."

"That last scene was beautiful," Dave said mistily.

"You really liked it, didn't you? As much as I did?" I was amazed. Most guys I'd met just weren't that romantic.

"Sure." He gazed at me with amusement. "What did you think, that I was some hard-core macho man?"

"No, more like a nuts-and-bolts historian type," I replied.

He laughed. "For your information, all historians are romantics. The past is very romantic."

"I'd never thought of it that way," I said.

"Since we're in a romantic mood," Dave suggested, "let's go to Nancy's and have a snack." Nancy's is an old-fashioned place with dim lighting, and it's quiet even on weekends.

There were a number of empty tables at Nancy's. Dave and I sat near the back of the dining room, where it was the most private and cozy. "I love this restaurant," I remarked, settling into my seat.

He reached for my hand. "And we can hold hands across the table."

I smiled, and a shiver ran up my spine. What a perfect date this was turning out to be.

Dave ordered iced tea and a sandwich, and I had a salad and a Coke.

"What are you involved in at school?" Dave asked.

"A couple of clubs and my media class. I'm hoping to get into the high-school radio program in the fall," I told him. "How about you?"

"I'm in the student government. I was junior class president last year. I think I'm going to try to get a history club going this fall in my spare time. Not that I have much of that." He grinned, his eyes staring into mine. A jolt rushed through me. Why did I always shiver when he touched me or even looked at me? Melody would have said I was falling in love. Maybe I was.

The best part of the evening happened once we'd finished eating and walked outside into the cool night air to the parking lot. That was when Dave kissed me! It was a beautiful kiss, filled with tenderness.

I stroked the back of his neck, memorizing the way it felt. It was as if time stood still for that moment and there was nothing in the world except Dave and me. Finally we pulled apart. Dave grinned, smoothing a strand of hair from my cheek. "I feel transported," he whispered. "Yet we're still standing in the parking area."

"Seems to me we met in one," I said breathlessly.

"That's right. A memorable moment." His arm dropped to my waist, and we strolled to the car.

On the way home, we sang along with songs on the radio. It felt so wonderful to be with someone special. I'd forgotten how great it had been with Derek, how much I'd really treasured those moments.

"Where do you live, Dave?" I asked as he swung into my driveway.

"Across town," he said, but didn't offer any more information. He cut the engine, and before I could form my next question, his arms were around me, his lips brushing mine one more time. For an instant I wondered if he was being deliberately vague, but his kisses canceled out any of my thoughts. What difference did it make, anyway?

"I know I shouldn't say this to you, Sammi," he whispered very seriously. "But good luck on the next show."

I giggled. "Same to you, Dave—don't tell anybody."

I skipped into the house and watched from the living room window until the car's taillights disappeared down the dark road. Then I got ready for bed, thinking that it would be strange playing against Dave on the next show.

Chapter Five

I should have known word would get out about Dave and me. But everything just felt so right between us that I hadn't really thought about it. I did feel a little annoyed, though, when Desiree Whitney brought the subject up while I was combing my hair in the restroom before the next "Brain Game." "I heard you went out with David Handlin," she commented, fluffing up her pretty blond hair with an Afro pick.

"Yes, I did." I smiled, but not too much because I didn't want her to know how much I liked him. Besides, it really wasn't any of her business whom I dated.

"Do you think that's wise?" she inquired in a low voice.

I stopped combing my hair to look at her. "I don't see why it wouldn't be wise, Desiree. We're playing a game, but what we do outside the show doesn't have anything to do with what goes on inside."

"I guess not," she said. "It just looks funny."

I shrugged, feeling suddenly less confident and a little defensive. "I can't help how it looks," I said, picking up my shoulder bag and walking out of the restroom. I felt hot and angry, and I wondered if Desiree had said that on purpose to upset me before the game.

Furious, I strode into the studio cafeteria, biting my lip to hold back my tears. I looked for Mel. She was the one person I went to when I felt confused or hurt. There she was, leaning against the Coke machine, talking to Shelley, who'd come to watch the game.

"Melody, I've got to talk to you. Could you excuse us, Shelley?" I asked.

"Well, sure," she answered, blinking in surprise.

We found a table in the corner, and I told Melody what had happened. "Sammi," she responded, "don't pay attention to Desiree. I don't think she's trying to bug you before the game. She could just be curious, not meaning any harm."

"That's true." But the whole incident left a sour taste in my mouth. I didn't want something petty to come between Dave and me.

I took a few deep breaths, and by the time we filed onto the set, I felt calmer and more relaxed.

45

Once we were seated, Dave smiled at me and waved. "Hi, Sammi. You look great," he called to me, indicating my pink sweat shirt dress and rhinestone necklace.

"Thanks." I returned the smile. My anger at Desiree was dissolving under the tenderness of those soft gray eyes.

Ty took his place between the teams and smiled reassuringly at us. He turned to the audience and addressed them. "Here we are for the second game of 'The Brain Game,' featuring the Wembley Giants and the Rushmore Royals. We're going to launch into some warm-up questions so that the teams can get ready to tear each other to shreds!" Everyone giggled. It was fun when Ty said things that he wouldn't say on the air. "First question, what did Ulysses Grant die of?"

Melody hit her buzzer. "Alcoholism?"

"No, wrong answer. Rushmore?"

A long silence, then the time buzzer followed. "The correct answer is cancer. If we'd been playing a game, that would have been a no score." Ty riffled through his blue cards. "Who wrote, 'No man is an island, entire of itself. . .'?"

"John Donne," replied Ophelia.

"Correct answer. Name the arena in Rome that served as the site of ancient sporting events."

I pressed my buzzer. "The Coliseum."

"That's correct. Name the gender and species of the largest whale."

Alan pressed his buzzer. "The female blue whale."

"That's correct. OK, we're one minute from show time now. Remember, the rules are the same, but we're minus a player on each team and will be down to three per team after tonight. Our opening will begin just about—" Ty's hand dropped, and he mouthed the word *now*.

The theme music rippled over the set. Dave smiled at me, the bright overhead lights cast a glow over his features. I returned his smile, then looked away as I remembered how wonderful it was to feel the brush of his lips against mine.

"Welcome, folks, to the second match of 'The Brain Game,' where we witness a battle of wits between our two competing schools, Rushmore and Wembley. The two schools are competing for five thousand dollars in prize money, which is to be used by the winning school to enrich academic programs. In addition, there is a five-thousand-dollar individual prize. For those of you unfamiliar with our game rules, each question is worth ten points . . ." Ty went through his regular speech, then we introduced ourselves.

"Everyone is just raring to go," Ty said. "We have four players per team tonight. Now, we'll begin with this question. The ancient Olympic pentathlon consisted of five separate contests. For ten points each, name two."

Dave buzzed. "Running and the discus throw."

"Correct." The Rushmore crowd clapped. "The other contests were the broad jump, javelin throw, and wrestling. Twenty points for Rushmore to Wembley's zero. Name the musical play in which the two rival gangs, the Sharks and the—"

Melody interrupted the question. "*West Side Story.*"

"*West Side Story* is correct, and the other rival gang I didn't mention is the Jets. The play updates the Shakespearean tragedy *Romeo and Juliet.*"

I flashed Melody a smile. Interrupting questions and getting them right was becoming a habit for her.

Ty picked up the next blue card. "The computer is capable of two kinds of memory, ROM and RAM. For ten points each, what do those acronyms stand for?"

Desiree Whitney replied: "ROM is Read-Only Memory, and RAM is Random-Access Memory."

"Correct answer. Forty points for Rushmore to Wembley's ten. The storage capacity for a computer is measured in bits and bytes. How many bits to a byte?"

Alan buzzed. "Eight."

"That's right, Alan. Twenty points for Wembley to Rushmore's forty." Ty took a deep breath, then continued with the next question. "The heart is a pump, divided into four major chambers. What are the upper and lower chambers called?"

Ron replied: "Aorta and centricles."

"Wrong answer. Wembley?"

Melody faltered. "Ventricles and—" Then the warbling time buzzer went off.

"Sorry, no point on that one. If any of you are going to be doctors, I hope you find out the answer to that one before you operate on me!" A few chuckles erupted from the audience. "The answer, folks, is atria and ventricles. OK, next question. Metals are good conductors of heat. Certain gases and liquids are not. What scientific term is used to describe substances that are poor conductors?"

"Insulators," replied Alan Whitlaw, pushing a lock of hair from his eyes.

A voice, which sounded suspiciously like Alan's younger brother's, called out of the audience, "Go, Alan!"

"Nice cheering squad," Ty said to Alan, who turned bright red. "The score is now thirty to forty in Rushmore's favor. We're going to take a short break now and return with the second round of 'The Brain Game.' "

It was nice to have a rest. I think we all needed

49

it. We were feeling the pressure of having one less team member. I thought about how hard it would be to sit up there, alone, staring at a single opponent. Hard, definitely. But did I ever want to be the one to try it!

The second part of the show began with a twenty-point question. "Wembley, here's your chance to pass Rushmore, if you can answer both parts of this question," said Ty. "Conduction is one method of heat transfer, name two others."

"Convection and radiation," Ron Bedford replied.

"Two correct answers for Rushmore, bringing the score up to sixty for Rushmore, thirty for Wembley. And here's a chance for Wembley to gain twenty points, if they answer this double question correctly. There was an essay published in New England in 1849 that advised people not to obey a law if they felt it was unjust. Name the essay, for ten points, and the author, for another ten points."

"Henry David Thoreau," I replied. "And the essay was . . ." I stalled not knowing the answer.

Thankfully, neither did Rushmore. "Ten points for Wembley for answering half the question. Thoreau is correct, and the essay that he wrote was entitled 'Civil Disobedience.' " Another ten points clacked up on the scoreboard, bringing us up to forty points; Rushmore was still ahead by twenty points.

Ty read off the next question. "A man walked one mile north, three miles west, then five miles south. How far is he from his starting point? You may use your scratch pads for this."

Desiree hit her buzzer a split second before Alan. "Five miles," she replied. Alan balled his hand into a fist because he knew the answer, too.

"Another ten points for Rushmore, bringing their total up to seventy points to Wembley's forty." I, personally, was feeling tired, but I was pulled along by Ty's enthusiasm. "All right, during which year did the Mayflower reach Plymouth Rock?"

"In 1620," replied Jessie, beaming.

"Ten points for Wembley, bringing that team up to fifty points. "Where did the Pilgrims first land?"

Dave answered. "Cape Cod, Provincetown."

A row of goose pimples erupted along my arms as I looked at him. Dave grinned at me for an instant before we both dropped our gazes to concentrate on the next question.

"This is our last question before our second break today," Ty said. "What union covers shirt-waist workers in this country?"

Dave beat Jessie on the buzzer, but then just

before he answered, a look of uncertainty crossed his face. "Garment workers," he said.

"Incomplete answer, I'm afraid, Dave. Perhaps the Wembley team can elaborate for us?" Ty turned to us.

Jessie replied, "The International Ladies Garment Workers Union."

"That is correct, Wembley earns another ten points to bring their score to sixty points to Rushmore's eighty. Stay tuned for our final segment, but first, here are some interesting facts about our schools."

The film began as Ty turned to Dave and said, "You almost had that last question."

"Yeah, I know," he said. "I had the abbreviation ILGWU in my mind but couldn't remember what all the letters stood for."

"You gave me just enough time to remember what they stood for," Jessie said, grinning.

As I looked at Dave, I wondered if he'd broken his concentration because he'd been thinking of me. Well, that only showed how careful I'd have to be about daydreaming. It was deadly for the game. *Think harder, Sammi*, I urged myself. I'd only answered one question so far that day. I needed to attack the game seriously!

Ty stacked his blue cards in front of him, then motioned for all of us to be quiet. "We're going back on the air now," he said, then put on a huge grin and addressed the cameras and audience. "Welcome back to the last portion of 'The Brain Game.' We're about to determine the winner of tonight's competition. Our teams are the Rushmore Royals and the Wembley Giants. Right now Rushmore is ahead with eighty points to Wembley's sixty. But, as you know, that lead could be turned around easily. On with the show. What year was the Magna Carta signed?"

I pressed my buzzer. "In 1215." I knew that from a history report I'd done on medieval women.

"Correct, Sammi. Who was the only supreme court justice appointed by Gerald Ford?"

I pressed my buzzer again. "Earl Warren?"

"No, incorrect answer. Good guess, though."

Dave buzzed. "John Stevens."

Ty glanced questioningly at the Judge, Mr. Krupp, who nodded his approval. "John Paul Stevens is the correct answer," Mr. Krupp replied, sending the Rushmore section into a wild frenzy. Lucinda had a hard time quieting them down.

Ty went on. "Ninety points for Rushmore and seventy for Wembley. Next question, when glucose is oxidized, what products result?"

Desiree answered, "Carbon dioxide, energy, and water."

"That is correct, Rushmore, bringing that

team's score up to one hundred to Wembley's seventy."

I glanced with concern at Alan. As our science whiz, he should have gotten that question. He shrugged helplessly at me. Maybe he was nervous or just plain tired. Anyway, none of us was doing too well that day. I was beginning to get a sinking feeling about this game. "Next question," Ty continued. "Who wrote a book called *Silent Spring*?"

Melody replied, "Rachel Carson."

"Correct answer for Wembley, giving that team eighty points to Rushmore's one hundred." That lifted my spirits a little.

"Joseph Smith organized the Church of the Latter-Day Saints in Fayette, New York, on April 6, 1830," Ty continued. "What common name is that organization also known by?"

Ron buzzed. "Mormons," he replied.

"Correct answer! Ten points for Rushmore, bringing the score to one hundred ten points to Wembley's eighty. Next question. Where is this group based today?"

Ron hit his buzzer again. "New York."

"Incorrect answer. How about Wembley giving this one a try?"

Jessie shrugged. "Salt Lake City, Utah?" he asked, looking uncertain.

"Correct answer, Jessie," Ty said. "That may

have been a guess, but you've just added another ten points to your score."

"Now, what federal agency currently monitors safety in the work place?"

Alan buzzed. "OSHA."

"That is correct. The Occupational Safety and Health Administration, known as OSHA. The score is now one hundred ten to one hundred, Rushmore leading. What a competition, folks! And now, listen closely, contestants, I have the last question of tonight's show. If Wembley gets it, we'll go into a three-question tie breaker. If Rushmore knows the answer, they'll win this game. Here it is! The Triangle Shirtwaist fire broke out on March 25, 1911. As a result, one hundred and forty-five people died, but an important social movement gained impetus, too. What was this movement?"

I hit my buzzer quickly. This one I knew for sure from my history class this year. "Unions—unionization." I said.

Ty glanced at Bill Krupp. "That's correct," Bill assured him. Unionization or the labor movement."

The crowd went wild, and so did I. I'd done it! I'd given my team a second chance to win the game. "All right, Sammi," Jessie called to me. It took Lucinda a good three minutes to get everyone quiet. There was more excitement and energy in that little room than on a basketball court during overtime. Finally the audience did settle down.

"This is what I call a great game," said Ty enthusiastically. "For any of you who have just tuned in to our show, I'm here with the Wembley Giants and the Rushmore Royals. With a brilliant answer by Sammi Edwards, the Wembley team has just pushed us to a tie breaker. Now we have three questions for you. Two correct answers give you the game. Are you ready? William the Conqueror fought and won a battle in 1066 and proclaimed himself king of England. Where was that battle?"

There was a moment of silence. Then Dave buzzed. "Hastings," he said definitively.

"Correct! If Rushmore answers this next tie breaker question, the game is theirs."

Think, Sammi, think, I commanded myself. *Don't let them win this game.* I concentrated on Dave's handsome face. This time I forced myself not to see him as a boy I liked and cared about, but only as a competitor.

Ty read the next question. "An organized women's rights movement was started in 1848 by five women in Seneca Falls, New York. Name two of them."

I went for my buzzer. It was a question made for me. "Elizabeth Cady Stanton and Mary Ann McClintock." Those individualistic women were my heroines.

"Yes!" Ty cried. "The other three were Lucretia Mott, her sister Martha Wright, and Jane Hurt. We're back at a tie. This last question will decide the game!"

I stared fixedly at Dave, and he stared back at me. It was as if we were locked in a battle of wits between just the two of us. We were both equally determined to win.

"The question is—name two Marx Brothers films."

Dave and I both went for our buzzers, but he got to his first. "*A Night at the Opera* and *A Day at the Races*," he cried.

"Correct!" The crowd went wild as a studio light swept over the Rushmore team. I just looked at Dave. He smiled at me and nodded his head once, as if acknowledging the competition I'd given him. As for me, I didn't feel too bad. I'd tried hard and done well. And there were still three more games for Wembley to win. "We'll beat you next time," I mumbled under my breath.

Ty spoke to the cameras over the cheering of the crowd. "Our big winners tonight are the Rushmore Royals. Last week Wembley was our victor. Next week we'll see these two teams battle it out again, minus a player each. The game will be even rougher, with only three players per team. Until next time, this is Ty Carlin, bidding you farewell from 'The Brain Game'!" The strains

of Vivaldi filled the small studio, and finally Ty
motioned that we were free to leave our seats.

Immediately Dave was surrounded by teammates and friends. After all, he'd won the game
for Rushmore. I stayed in my seat and watched
him talking animatedly with the others. He was
really a genius. I mean, everyone on "The Brain
Game" was smart, and we all were students recognized for academic achievement. But Dave
was different, special. He was so quick, and he
knew so much.

After a moment he glanced up and noticed me
looking at him. He grinned and gave me the
thumbs-up signal. Then he mouthed the words,
You're a winner. No one else saw it, but it made
my heart sing.

Just then, I became aware of Melody standing
in the doorway, looking very upset. I stood up
and went to her. "What's wrong, Mel?"

"Don't you know, Sammi?" Tears leaked out
the corners of her eyes. "I won't be back on the
game. I answered the fewest questions for
Wembley."

"Oh, no," I cried. "Melody, I'm sorry."

"I guess I just wasn't concentrating today.
But, Sammi, you were fantastic. You almost won
the game for us."

"I came close, but not close enough, I'm afraid.
Who else is out?"

"Ophelia Long. You know it seems awfully

unfair, and yet, of course, I know it's how the game is played."

I jumped when I felt a warm hand on my shoulder. I spun around to find Dave gazing into my eyes. "Will you two be at Cleo's?" he wanted to know.

"Um—" I hesitated as I looked at Melody, who nodded. "Yes, we're going."

"Good. See you there."

"Oh, uh, Dave," I said casually, "you were great. Congratulations."

"Thanks, so were you. Quite a competition. You certainly are a challenge, Sammi." He nodded, then turned and jogged to catch up with the other members of his team.

"Come on," I said to Melody. "Let's go celebrate—I mean, go soothe our wounds. We don't want Rushmore to think we're sore losers."

"No, only disappointed ones. I guess Shelley and I can cry in our Cokes together."

"I really wished that you and I would be the last ones on the show," I told her.

"Yeah, well, that's one wish of yours that won't come true, Sammi," she said. "But you've got other wishes in your head. Maybe you'll have better luck with them."

We wandered out to the parking lot and drove over to Cleo's. I thought about Dave all the way there.

Chapter Six

"Have you been friends with Melody a long time?" Dave asked me. We were stuck in a corner of Cleo's next to the jukebox, and we had to talk very loudly. Melody had insisted on sitting with Shelley and Alan, leaving Dave and me alone.

"Since third grade," I replied, sipping my ice-cream soda.

"I could tell it was a long-term friendship. You two seem awfully close."

"Like sisters. Maybe even closer. Sisters fight more than we do."

"Boy, do I know! I have three of them. They gang up on me, too, being the only boy." He sighed and munched a few french fries.

"Poor thing," I said soothingly. "But you must understand women pretty well, living with so many of them."

"Hmmmm, maybe. Mostly it makes me very

patient because I always have to wait for the bathroom in the morning. I'm about the most patient guy I know."

"That's a good quality," I said. "I'm about the most *impatient* person I know. I can't wait for anything. Like getting my driver's license. Or winning 'The Brain Game.' "

He grinned. A few tables over Melody laughed with Shelley and Alan. "Melody doesn't seem too upset now," observed Dave, finishing off the fries.

"She doesn't brood," I explained. "I would probably throw a fit. I like to win."

"Don't we all. But everyone has got to lose sometime."

"I hope I don't," I said unrealistically. "Well, I don't want to reveal any more of my bad qualities," I added, joking.

"So far, I've seen only your good ones. You'll have to tell me about the bad ones. Otherwise, I'll never notice them."

"It's nice to know I'm putting my best face forward," I returned happily. Wow, this was incredible. Dave and I were really falling for each other.

Dave glanced at his watch. "Wow, it's late. I've got to go, Sammi. I'm tutoring a kid, and I have to get ready for him."

"Does he watch 'The Brain Game'?" I asked.

"Oh, yeah, he's faithful. He wants to be just like me."

61

"Striving for perfection, maybe?" I quipped.

Dave laughed. "Are you watching the airing of the first show?" he asked me.

"You bet."

"Great, think of me." He gave my hand a squeeze and pushed his way through the crowd to the door. He waved as he pushed the door open.

Melody and I left a short while later in her car. "I'm feeling better," she confided.

"Good. I knew a little socializing would help your blues."

"It'll be almost as good for me if you win, Sammi," she said.

"Keep rooting for me," I said. "Hey, how about coming for dinner? It'll be no fun going home to eat with only Kate tonight." Our parents were out to dinner.

"Love to. That'll help make a perfectly horrible day a bit better," she said.

After supper we settled down with the papers. "Maybe I should get a job just so I can search for one with you," I suggested as we pored over the want ads.

Melody shot me a dirty look. "There aren't enough jobs around for you to have that luxury," she said. "Look, here's a baby-sitting position. 'Cute four-year-old needs intelligent, calm, neat sitter.' That's me!" Melody dialed the number and talked to a woman who had an accent. They et up an appointment to talk after the woman's ennis lesson the next day. She hung up and urned to me with a big smile. "She seems nice. .nd I think if I'm employed, I'll feel a lot better bout losing the game," she reflected.

"Everything will fall into place for you, Mel. ust wait and see." I hugged her. That's the way : is with us. We can always tell when the other eeds a little TLC. I can't count the times Melo- y's helped me get back together after some near isaster in my life. "Why don't you spend the ight?" I asked her. "Then we can watch the rst taping of the show together."

"If it's all right, that'd be great."

"You know it is." Mom had accepted Melody as 1ough she were one of her own daughters.

Just then the phone rang. Katie answered it rst and called down the hall to me, "Sammi, it's or you!" When I went to take the phone from er, she hissed in my ear, "It's a boy." I rolled my yes at her, but she simply grinned and waited) hear what I said.

"Hello?"

"Hi. How are you, Sammi?" Dave asked.

"Oh, fine—just about the same as when I last aw you."

He laughed. "Is Melody OK?"

"Yes, she's spending the night here."

"Do you stay up all night giggling and ılking?"

"No, we're deadly serious," I quipped, and h
chuckled. I loved the sound of his laugh. "Hov
was your tutoring session?" I asked.

"Fine. Nate is doing much better on his math
I really enjoy teaching him."

"That's neat. How long have you had the job?"

"About a year. We really like each other. I
almost doesn't feel like a job at all."

I felt a twinge of guilt. I guessed that Dave ha
worked a lot of jobs during his life. I really didn
have much to say on the subject since all I'd eve
done was a little baby-sitting. Of course, I did m
share around the house, but that wasn't pai
employment. I knew I was a very lucky girl.

"I was wondering if you had plans for tomo
row," Dave said. His voice caught in midser
tence, but then he continued smoothly. Mayb
he was a little nervous. He didn't need to be. I
cherished the idea of going out with him agair
In fact, I was ecstatic.

"My only plans are to go shopping with Me
ody," I replied. "We're getting her ears pierced.

"Would you like to go to a party at Tedd
Cummings's house?" he asked.

I tried not to sound too eager, but I could fe
my excitement bursting to get out. "Oh, I'd lov
to. What time?"

"It starts around eight, but you know ho
those things go. We'll want to be fashionab!

late. I'll pick you up just before eight, if that's OK."

"OK," I said happily.

"Don't forget to watch us on TV, Sammi," he reminded me before hanging up.

When I hung up the phone, I turned around to find both Melody and Katie standing behind me grinning. "What are you waiting for?" Melody asked. "What did he say?"

"Didn't you two eavesdroppers hear enough already?" I asked, pretending to be very annoyed.

"No!" said Katie truthfully. "So you better help us out."

"OK, OK," I said. "Dave asked me to a party."

Melody's violet eyes widened. "Oh, that's the best thing that's happened today," she cried, hugging me.

"Aren't you crossing enemy lines?" Katie frowned at me.

"How can you think such a thing, Katie? What difference does it make?" I cried.

"You never know," she said ominously, shaking her head. She glanced at her watch. "Hey, it's almost eight, time for the first 'Brain Game.' "

"All right!" I said, perfectly happy to avoid Katie's dire warnings about Dave and me. "Let's get something cold to drink while we watch."

Five minutes later Mom and Dad dashed in, and we sat down in the living room, ready for the game. Ty's smiling face came on the screen after the Vivaldi theme music poured into the room. It was incredible seeing myself on TV. Everyone had told me the cameras would put ten pounds on me, but I didn't appear that way at all. Frankly, I thought I looked great. And I seemed much sharper and quicker than I'd felt in the studio. I noticed the same things about Melody.

I really enjoyed watching Dave. He was even more handsome on TV. But best of all, I could see how many times he glanced at me.

"He looks at you a lot, Sammi," Melody whispered.

"I never realized that when we were on the set," I whispered back.

"Just imagine, a romance blossoms on TV, right before our eyes," said Melody, keeping her voice low so my family wouldn't hear. "Someday we'll read about this in the *Enquirer*."

"Not if I can help it," I growled, never taking my eyes off the screen. It was wonderful being able to stare at Dave without interruption.

Chapter Seven

"This is going to be good therapy for you." I was trying to convince Melody as we got into her car. We were headed for the mall to get her ears pierced. "You need an uplift, and you've wanted to get this done for a long time."

"True." Melody kept her eyes on the driveway as she backed out. "But I'm still scared."

"You won't feel a thing. They put the earring into a hole puncher type of machine and they punch it right into your ear. It happens so fast you won't even know it. Of course, we could save ten dollars and do it at home with a needle and an ice cube," I suggested, rolling down the window to let some cool air in.

"I'll pass on that idea," she said. "I guess I'm as ready as I'll ever be."

I had my ears pierced when I was about ten, which sent my father into an absolute fit. Of course, he's over it now. When Mom had hers done a couple of years ago, he gave up on us both, and I don't think he's even noticed that Katie has them, too.

To get Mel's mind off the upcoming ear piercing, I started talking about Dave. "Isn't Dave wonderful on TV?" I asked, sighing.

"Yes, but so is everybody else," she reminded me. "Watch those stars in your eyes, Sammi. Hey, by the way, Desiree told me he's from a poor family and he wants to win so that he won't have to work so much while he's in college."

"He has to work while he's in college?" I gasped. Most of my friends planned to have summer jobs while going to college to help out with costs, but none of them would need to work during the school year.

"Yes. Desiree said he worked two jobs last year to save money." She turned the car onto the main road.

"He tutors someone," I mumbled, feeling very sorry for him. "He never told me any of this."

"Why would he tell you, Sammi? He wouldn't want you to feel sorry for him. He knows what kind of home you come from. Those are just the breaks as far as he's concerned."

"Yeah. I do a lot of complaining about my parents, but I do fine. Dave probably wishes he had it as easy as I do."

"Desiree says Dave's got a great family. There

are four kids in the family, and he's the only boy. Can you imagine?"

"He told me." I was quiet for a minute, thinking about his situation. "Gee, wanting a car seems pretty frivolous," I said, patting the seat, "compared to wanting an education, doesn't it?"

"You're lucky. So am I," Melody commented. "Our parents can give us just about anything we really need. Here we are," she said, pulling into the mall parking area.

"This helps me understand Dave better," I said aloud. Then I mumbled, "No wonder he didn't want me to know exactly where he lived."

"What?" Melody asked as she stopped the car.

"Oh, nothing. Just muttering to myself."

We entered the shopping mall and headed straight for the jewelry counter of Macy's. A woman told us about a special deal, free ear piercing with the purchase of a pair of real gold earrings. I helped Melody pick out the right ones, small gold shells.

"And now for the surgery," Melody said with a grimace.

"Be brave," I said, encouragingly.

Another woman behind the counter led us to a room where they did the piercing. She put the earrings into the hole-puncher-type machine I had told Melody about. I felt momentarily relieved that it wasn't happening to me, even though I knew it wouldn't hurt. Melody sat down stiffly. She really looked scared as the woman raised the machine to her ear and she closed her eyes.

"Did it happen yet?" she asked after a moment.

"Yes, the left ear is done," the woman said.

"Wow. I hardly felt it. Did you feel it, Sam?" She immediately burst into giggles when she realized what she had asked.

"Not yet. I'll take you out for a stiff drink afterward." The saleswoman frowned at me, so I added, "A stiff drink of ginger ale." Melody giggled again.

"All done," the saleswoman said, standing back to check out her handiwork. "Your earrings are in. Now aren't you lovely?"

We scrutinized Melody's reflection in the small stand-up mirror. "Lovely," we chorused, then cracked up. At least the holes were even. I couldn't have guaranteed that if I'd done them with ice and a needle.

We strolled out of Macy's and found an ice-cream parlor, where we ordered root beer floats. Then we browsed around in a jewelry shop, looking at the earrings. I bought a pair of bright pink, metallic, dangly earrings. I wondered if Dave ever treated himself to whatever boys treat themselves to, T-shirts, sneakers, records, and stuff. I wondered if he got an allowance or if he earned all his money working. He seemed generous enough with me, treating me to the movies and snacks. Suddenly I was worried about his finances. Maybe I should offer to pay my way sometimes.

"Do you ever go dutch when you go out on a date?" I asked Melody.

"Oh, sure, especially when we're getting something expensive like concert tickets."

Hmm, I thought as we left the shop and strolled toward the parking lot. I never realized I might be making things tough for Dave. Well, I'd have to be more sensitive in the future.

I was still thinking about Dave not having a lot of money when he came to pick me up for the party. As we were driving toward Teddy's house, I found myself scrutinizing his clothes for frays. I didn't find any. His clothes weren't new, but they weren't shabby either.

"You're looking at me funny tonight, Sammi. What's up? Never seen a winner before?"

"I've seen plenty of them," I answered. "But none of them look as good as you. Are you and Desiree friends?" I inquired, wondering why she knew so much about him.

"Not really, but she lives down the street from me. We've known each other since we were kids. I took her to a dance when we were in eighth grade because she wanted to go so much, but otherwise, we're not too friendly. Why?"

"Just wondering."

"Did she say something to you?" he quizzed me. One thing I was beginning to notice about Dave—he didn't let anything go by him. He asked a lot of questions.

"Not much," I replied. He looked at me out of the corner of his eye, and I smiled, ignoring the look. "Well, if it helps," he said, with a sly grin, "she's known as a big mouth and a gossip."

"Oh, I could've guessed," I said.

Desiree's news made me look at everything about Dave differently, even his car, which was kind of old. I noticed every little rattle as he drove to the party. I wanted to be useful to him. He was so smart, and I was so much more fortunate than he was where money was concerned. What if he couldn't get a big scholarship and go to college? What if he couldn't save enough to make it happen for himself? With four kids in his family and not a lot of income, he might have trouble. As we approached Teddy's, I pushed my thoughts to the back of my mind. I knew this was no time for gloominess.

The place was ablaze with lights. Japanese lanterns were strung across the front porch of the modern two-story home, and dance music blared out from the house. Teddy greeted us at the door. "Hi, Dave, hi, Sammi. Our two star players exchanging notes, huh?"

"Uh, I don't think so, Teddy," Dave replied.

shaking his head. "Sammi and I are dating, but we're not really discussing the game." I liked the way that sounded. *"Sammi and I are dating . . ."* I repeated it in my mind a few times, reveling in the rhythm of those words.

Dave and I strolled downstairs to the family room, where a group of kids were lounging around a pool table. I recognized some people from Rushmore. Ophelia Long and Desiree Whitney were there, talking with two dark-haired boys. Ron Bedford and a few others were playing Trivial Pursuit on a card table in the corner.

A Michael Jackson song came on the stereo, and Dave turned to me. "Do you want to dance?" he asked.

"Love to." He took my hand and led me to the middle of the floor, where a couple was already dancing. It was a fast song, and Dave held my fingers and twirled me under his arm. I felt dizzy, happy, and not ready to stop when the song ended. After that came a slow number, and Dave hugged me closely and glided us around the floor, guiding my movements with his body. I shivered at the sensation of his hand against the small of my back, and the pleasant pressure of his cheek against mine. He swung me around, my hair flowing out behind me in an auburn arc. I wished that the dance could last forever.

I heard a few people whisper about us as we

passed. *Let them whisper*, I thought, closing my eyes and swaying gently against Dave's body. Nothing mattered then, not the other kids, not the game—only Dave.

Chapter Eight

"And on our Rushmore team, we have David Handlin, Ron Bedford, and Desiree Whitney. Sammi Edwards, Allan Whitlaw, and Jessie Klein comprise the Wembley team. Now if you'll introduce yourselves, gang," Ty started off with his usual introduction, and we each in turn gave a short summary of our accomplishments and goals. He explained the rules for new viewers and then launched into the first battery of questions.

David smiled at me, but I kept my eyes away from him. "Now keep those fingers on the buzzers, contestants, and we'll begin the questions. Who wrote *The Adventures of Huckleberry Finn*?"

I buzzed. "Mark Twain."

"Ten points for Wembley," Ty said, and the scoreboard clacked up my ten points. "What

75

food sustains a hibernating animal during the winter?"

Dave buzzed. "It lives on stored fat," he replied.

"That's correct, bringing Rushmore even with Wembley. Name the baroque composer who wrote a concerto grosso entitled *The Four Seasons*."

Jessie Klein hit his buzzer. "Vivaldi."

"Antonio Vivaldi is correct, and he is also the composer of our theme music on this program," Ty replied. "Wembley now has twenty points to Rushmore's ten. OK, next question. What country celebrates an October revolution?"

Desiree buzzed. "Russia."

"That's correct. The USSR, or Russia, celebrates an October revolution. Rushmore and Wembley are tied again at twenty points each. Next, name the calendar adopted by the Bolsheviks that changed the anniversary of the October revolution to November?"

Jessie pressed his buzzer. "The Gregorian calendar."

"That's right. Thirty points for Wembley. In the fall, leaves stop producing a certain substance, which allows the other colors, always present, to become visible. Name this substance."

Alan buzzed. "Chlorophyll."

"Correct answer for Wembley. The score is forty to twenty, Wembley leading. Next, contestants, name the pigment responsible for coloring leaves yellow."

Alan buzzed. "Carotenoids."

"Another correct answer for Wembley, bringing the score to fifty points for that team and twenty for Rushmore. In 1972 a black woman ran for president of the United States. Who was she?"

I hit my buzzer fast, just before Dave got to his. "Shirley Chisholm," I responded.

"Yes! The score is sixty for Wembley to Rushmore's twenty as we break at the end of the first portion of our game tonight. Folks, we have two great high schools contending. Here's a description of the schools themselves, and we'll be back with you in a moment for 'The Brain Game.' "

I leaned back in my chair. Dave smiled at me. I sort of wished he wouldn't. It made me remember what it was like to dance in his arms, and that certainly didn't make for good concentration. Still, I returned the smile feebly, wishing he wasn't on the opposite team.

After the film Ty took a deep breath and began speaking again. "Welcome back to the second part of 'The Brain Game.' OK, teams, get ready for the next question. The words *aquifer, aquaduct,* and *aquamarine* all contain the prefix *aqua*. What does *aqua* mean?"

Dave buzzed. "Water."

"That is correct, Dave. Rushmore now has

thirty points to Wembley's sixty. Continuing on that subject, what literary character complained, 'Water, water everywhere, nor any drop to drink'?"

"The old man in *The Old Man and the Sea*?" questioned Ron.

"No, Ron, that's not it."

I buzzed. "Coleridge's the Ancient Mariner."

"That's correct. Ten points for Wembley, giving that team seventy points to Rushmore's thirty. OK, teams, approximately June twenty second marks the summer solstice in the U.S. What does it denote in Australia?"

Ron buzzed. "Winter solstice."

"That is correct—another ten points for the Rushmore Royals. Rushmore forty, Wembley seventy."

I glanced over at Dave and found him staring directly at me. He seemed a little slow that day as if he were thinking about something other than the game. Maybe me. *Come on, don't day dream*, I found myself silently urging him.

"OK," Ty went on, "what biochemical process slows in order to conserve energy during hibernation?"

Alan buzzed. "The metabolic rate," he replied.

"Correct answer from Wembley once more!" Ty waved his hand at the scoreboard as it tallied up our points. "Eighty for Wembley, forty for Rushmore. How many cups are there in a gallon?"

Dave buzzed. "Sixteen."

Good, I thought. *At least he's awake now.* Then I realized I'd been so busy worrying that Dave was off in another world that I'd completely missed the question. I yanked myself back to the game. Daydreaming was not what I wanted to be doing right then.

"All right, contestants," Ty said. "You may use your scratch pads for this one. How many gallons of water must be added to four gallons of a seventy-five percent acid solution to reduce the strength to twenty-five percent acid?" It was definitely not my kind of question, and I prayed quickly that Jessie or Alan would know. For a moment all I heard was the sound of pencils moving furiously over paper. Then Desiree buzzed. "Twelve."

"That is correct. Ten points for Desiree's team, sixty in all for Rushmore, and eighty for Wembley. What play, broadcast over the radio in October, 1938, caused a panic in the eastern U.S.?"

I buzzed. *"The War of the Worlds."*

By now the audience was screaming, and goose pimples traveled up my arms. "Correct answer, Sammi. Wembley now has ninety points, to Rushmore's sixty. Who wrote the novel on which this play was based?"

I buzzed for that one, too. "H.G. Wells," I answered, and our crowd cheered. Lucinda

waved them silent so Ty wouldn't have to shou
over the din.

"Another correct answer for Wembley. On
hundred points to Rushmore's sixty. We'v
reached the end of the second part of the show
folks, so we'll let them applaud freely fo
Wembley High, while we take a brief intermis
sion." As the cameras moved off us, he mu
tered, "Good game." I relaxed for a momen
thinking about how much more excited th
audience was with only three players. The gam
was beginning to be exhausting. And it woul
only get harder from now on. Being a finalis
sure would be tough. The break was over to
soon. And before I knew it, almost before I wa
ready, we were back in the middle of the game.

"Japan," Ty was saying, "established a dis
tinctive culture and civilization from the sev
enth to the ninth centuries A.D. What countr
served as the model for Japan's economic an
political systems?"

Dave buzzed for that one. "China."

"China is correct. Rushmore is up to sevent
points to Wembley's one hundred. OK, Chin
became unified and began building the Grea
Wall in a particular dynasty. Which—?"

A buzzer went off before the end of the ser
tence. Ron answered. "The Ch'in."

"That's right. Rushmore is up to eighty point
to Wembley's one hundred. There are man

kinds of alphabets. In which alphabet will you find the letters alpha and beta?"

Jessie buzzed. "Greek," he replied.

Applause broke the silence. "Wembley's up to one hundred ten points. Rushmore's right behind at eighty." Ty flipped his blue cards. "By what name were Ethan Allen's rebels known?"

"The Green Mountain Boys," Dave replied.

"Ninety points for Rushmore, one hundred ten for Wembley. On to the next question. What do the words *vert* and *mont* mean in French?"

"Green Mountain," Jessie replied.

"That's right. The word *Vermont* means 'green mountain,' " Ty added. "That puts Wembley right up there at one hundred twenty points to ninety for Rushmore. In which state were the Martians in *The War of the Worlds* supposed to have landed?"

Jessie buzzed just before I did. "New York," he said.

"Wrong. Rushmore?"

"New Jersey," Ron replied.

"Correct answer. Rushmore has one hundred points to Wembley's one hundred twenty."

Darn, I thought. *We would have gotten those points if I'd been a little quicker.* It sure was frustrating to lose out to a teammate.

"In the 1960s American pop music was dominated by English artists. For ten points, name three bands that were part of this 'English Invasion.' "

This time I got to my buzzer fast. "The Beatles, the Rolling Stones, and the Who."

"Good, Sammi. To you, that may be ancient history," Ty said. "But I remember those bands when they first came to the U.S. The score is now one hundred thirty for Wembley, one hundred for Rushmore. For the last question of tonight's show, what is the scientific name for the human race?"

Ron buzzed. "Homo sapiens," he said.

"Correct, Ron. The score is one hundred thirty to one hundred ten, which means that Wembley High is the winner of tonight's show. Tune in next week when we're down to two players per team, the last game before the final play-off. Who will be Springfield's winning team? Join us and find out." The Vivaldi music started, eventually drowning out the audience's cheers.

As I stood up and moved away from my friends, Dave walked toward me. I smiled. "That was some game," I said.

"Congratulations. You were formidable."

"Thank you. So were you," I replied. "It was a tough competition."

"Well, would the champ be averse to a little refreshment with the leading loser?" He grinned.

"Sure," I said enthusiastically. "Just let me tell

my folks." Then I remembered something and added, "As long as you'll let me treat you this time."

Dave looked at me a little strangely, then said, "Why not? What more should I expect from a singular woman like you, Sammi?" And with that, he tucked his arm under mine.

Chapter Nine

I was terrified on the next "Brain Game." First of all because Jessie and I were pitted against Dave and Ron, who were a rough duo. But more importantly, whenever I had tried to quiz myself or study for the game, thoughts of Dave pulled me away from my studies. I had to consciously force myself to concentrate.

On the day of the game I quickly scanned through the latest issue of *Teen Town*. There was an interesting contest advertised. "Write an essay about a historical figure," I read. "First Prize—$1,000. To enter, submit an essay of from 1500 to 2000 words to this magazine about your favorite historical hero or heroine. Finalists will be notified by mail, and winners will be published in *Teen Town.*" I decided that might be fun to start thinking about, something interesting to work on after "The Brain Game."

I spent a long time poring over the contents of my closet, wondering what I could wear that Dave would like. *Now if this isn't distracted,* I thought, *I don't know what is.* I finally snatched a lavender shirt off its hanger, paired it with a purple skirt, and tied a scarf around my waist.

Later, when I walked into the studio, I caught up with Dave, who was standing by the drinking fountain. "Hey," I said, tapping him on the shoulder.

He turned, smiling. "Hi, Sammi. Good luck." Then he leaned over and kissed my cheek, his breath fluttering against my ear.

I shivered happily. "Thanks. Same to you."

I strode onto the set, feeling all quivery inside. My mom and dad waved at me from the bleachers as I took my place on stage, and I waved back with two fingers. Katie made a face at me, which I did not return, since too many people would have seen me doing it.

Jessie turned to me and squeezed my hand. "This is it, Sam. Good luck."

"You, too, Jessie. Boy, we'll really need it this game."

Ty said a few words to the audience, then read a few practice questions. "Just relax with these warm-up questions, teams. Save your strength for the long game ahead," he coached us. "Now, the words, *subway, submarine,* and *subter-*

reanean all contain the prefix *sub*. What does that prefix mean?"

Ron buzzed. "Under."

"That's correct. OK, what term is used to describe a sound whose frequency is inaudible?"

I buzzed. "Sonic?"

"No, wrong answer. Rushmore?" Both Dave and Ron shook their heads. "Looks like this one will have to pass, folks. The correct answer is subsonic." Ty shuffled through his cards. "Name the poet who said, 'I have promises to keep, and miles to go before I sleep.' "

"Robert Frost," I replied.

"Correct. With what group of poets is William Wordsworth associated?"

Dave buzzed for that one. "The Romantic poets."

"Very good. All right, we've got a couple of minutes until the competition starts. Make sure your fingers are on the buzzers, mikes in position." Ty watched Lucinda's face as she counted down the seconds. Then the music filtered through the studio. I looked up. Dave was watching me. He smiled, and I smiled back.

Ty's voice rose and fell as he introduced the game, the rules, and, finally, us. "We have two formidable teams pitted against each other tonight. After this game, one player on each team will be disqualified, leaving the last two players to battle it out to the finish on our next program of 'The Brain Game.' Five thousand dollars will rest on that contest. Now, are we ready to begin? First question, what early vehicle was known as 'the Iron Horse'?"

David buzzed. "Locomotive." Rushmore's fans cheered, and I could tell it was going to be an energetic game.

"That is correct, ten points for the Rushmore Royals, Wembley zero. OK, name the first American-built locomotive capable of hauling a payload."

Jessie buzzed. *"Tom Thumb."*

"That is correct. Wembley scores ten points, too. Next question, where did the first manned, powered airplane flight take place?"

David buzzed. "Kitty Hawk, North Carolina."

The Rushmore section hooted again. "That is correct. Twenty points now for Rushmore, and ten for Wembley." Ty motioned to Lucinda to quiet the crowd, which she did tactfully. "In what city was the first passenger airplane service started?"

Jessie buzzed. "Atlantic City."

"Correct answer, giving Wembley twenty points to Rushmore's twenty. What was the purpose of the Underground Railroad during the U.S. Civil War?"

I buzzed for that one. "To bring slaves north to the free states."

"That is correct, Sammi, giving your team

thirty points to Rushmore's twenty. Next question. Who was the famous female slave—?"

Dave buzzed. "Harriet Tubman."

"That is correct. Harriet Tubman was a famous female slave who served as a conductor on the Underground Railroad. This adds ten points to Rushmore's score, a thirty-to-thirty tie. This question is visual." Ty held up a photo. "This is a human embryo at twenty-four weeks. What name is given to the organism?"

Ron replied, "Fetus."

"That is correct. Forty points for Rushmore, thirty for Wembley." The audience screamed. "OK, last question in this round of 'The Brain Game.' The fetus is surrounded by a sac full of fluid. What is this fluid and sac called? One word."

"Amniotic," I replied, sending the Wembley crowd into a frenzy.

"That is correct, Wembley, you move up to forty points and tie the Rushmore Royals. We've come to the end of the first part of 'The Brain Game.' We'll take a look at our schools during this break." As the film ran, I doodled on my note pad while the other three talked because I didn't want to look at Dave. I needed a clear head, and looking at him tended to cloud my thinking.

"Welcome back to the second part of 'The Brain Game,'" Ty began after the film. "We're tied right now at forty points apiece for the Wembley

Giants and the Rushmore Royals. The first question of the second portion of our show is this. What are synfuels?"

Jessie replied. "They're fuels synthesized from things other than crude oil or natural gas."

Ty conferred briefly with Mr. Krupp before announcing that the answer was correct. "That gives Wembley a big fifty points to Rushmore's forty. Oil shale is one synfuel. What has to be done to the shale to extract the oil?"

"The shale must be heated or melted," answered Dave.

"Rushmore has answered correctly, giving that team fifty points. We're neck and neck now, folks." It seemed as though neither of our teams could pull ahead for more than one question. Ty continued. "One of the messengers of the gods was a young male whose symbol was winged sandals. The Romans called him Mercury. In Greek mythology—"

Jessie buzzed. "Hermes."

"That is correct, Jessie. Sixty points for Wembley, fifty for Rushmore. Another messenger of the gods is Iris. Her symbol is a multicolored road—"

I buzzed this time. "The rainbow."

"That is correct. The multicolored road Iris traveled to descend to earth was the rainbow. Another ten for Wembley, giving the team seventy points to Rushmore's fifty. Our next question is, again, visual." Ty held up a picture cut out of a magazine. "This picture is composed of little bits of colored stone. What is the name—?"

Ron buzzed. "Mosaic."

"Correct answer. The name of this ancient art form is mosaic, which gives Rushmore sixty points to Wembley's seventy. What ancient story is pictured here?"

Ty held up a picture of Noah's Ark.

All the buzzers went off, but Ron had gotten to his first. "Noah's Ark."

"Correct, Wembley and Rushmore are tied now at seventy points. And where is Noah's Ark believed to be located at this time?"

"Mount Ararat," I supplied.

"Sammi Edwards has just added ten points to Wembley's score, for a whopping eighty points to Rushmore's seventy. Now, what is the object, carried by the dove, which symbolizes peace?"

"Olive branch," I answered.

"Good work, Sammi. Ninety points for Wembley, seventy for Rushmore as we end the second portion of 'The Brain Game.' Stay tuned for the last part of our show."

Dave smiled at me shyly. An image of his kissing me the other night slipped into my mind. I quickly blotted it out as I heard Ty talking about our being only a minute from show time. I watched Dave rake his fingers through his glossy hair, and I thought of us dancing together. Then I stopped myself. Everything was going so well on the show, I didn't want to start thinking about that. *Concentrate, concentrate,* I told myself, hoping I could.

"Welcome back," Ty said. "Contestants, our next question is a math problem, so use your scratch pads. A one-mile-long train, traveling at sixty miles per hour, enters a two-mile-long tunnel at seven-oh-two. At what time will the last car leave the tunnel?"

There was a moment with only the sound of pencils on paper. I tried but knew I wasn't fast enough with math questions. Thank goodness, Jessie was the first to buzz. "Seven-oh-five," he replied.

"Correct answer. Jessie gives his team ten points to bring Wembley to one hundred points, seventy for Rushmore." Ty sifted through his cards. "Next question. U.S. spacemen are called astronauts, literally, 'star sailors.' What do Russians call their space explorers?"

"Cosmonauts," replied Ron.

"Correct answer," Ty exclaimed. "Rushmore eighty, Wembley one hundred. Who was the first woman to make a nonstop transatlantic flight?"

I buzzed for that one. "Amelia Earhart." She was one of my favorite heroines.

"Correct answer for Wembley. That team has one hundred ten points to Rushmore's eighty."

The Wembley section applauded enthusiastically while Ty went on to the next question. "Who made the first transatlantic *solo* flight?"

I answered again. "Charles Lindbergh."

Wembley's cheering section went absolutely crazy. "One hundred twenty points for Wembley, eighty points for Rushmore. A steam-powered engine that uses wood or coal to produce heat is an example of what kind of engine?"

Dave hit his buzzer. "External combustion engine."

The entire Rushmore section whooped with excitement. "Correct answer, Dave, for Rushmore. Ninety points for that team to one hundred twenty for Wembley. What kind of fuel does an internal combustion engine use?"

Dave buzzed. "Gaseous fuel."

"Correct," said Ty. "Next. In April, 1980, a regime was overthrown in the African country Rhodesia. What is that state now called?"

I hit my buzzer just before Dave hit his. "Zimbabwe."

"Correct," Ty said. "The score is one hundred thirty to one hundred, and Wembley's ahead. For tonight's last question, what branch of mathematics uses the terms 'sine,' 'cosine,' 'tangent,' and 'cotangent'?"

This time Dave buzzed first. "Trigonometry."

"Correct answer, giving Rushmore a big one hundred ten points, but not enough to beat

Wembley with their one thirty. Wembley Giants, you are the winners of this fourth game of the tournament. That means you've won three games. Even if Rushmore wins the next, you still are our team winners. Wembley High will receive five thousand dollars." The crowd went wild. "One player from each team will be dropped after tonight," Ty continued, "so we will have only one player on each side for the next 'Brain Game,' taped here at CAT Cable TV."

Lucinda walked onto the set and handed Ty a slip of paper. Our personal scores had already been tallied, and the note told which of us would continue. I crossed my fingers. "For our next game, we'll welcome back David Handlin of Rushmore High School and Sammi Edwards of Wembley. And to the rest of you, thanks so much for playing our game. We wish you the very best. Good night from 'The Brain Game.' "

I stared across the room at Dave and Ron. Dave was grinning from ear to ear. He leaped up from his seat as soon as Ty said it was OK to move, and he came straight over to me.

"Did you hear that, Sammi? We made it! We're contenders for the grand prize!" he cried out, grasping me in his strong embrace. I breathed in the sweet scent of his soap. All the self-control I'd exercised during the game dropped away, and I just let myself be surrounded by Dave's intoxicating warmth.

When I glanced out at the audience, I noticed a few people looking at us strangely. Then I realized how odd it must seem to them. Two opponents locked in a giant bear hug!

Chapter Ten

Mr. Carmalinghi turned off the Betamax and ran a hand through his hair. "Well, Sammi, you're as ready as you're ever going to be for the big day." We were sitting in his office on the second floor of Wembley High. It had a great view of the front of the school. Some kids were skateboarding down the sidewalk.

I sighed heavily. "I just don't feel ready, somehow."

"Confidence, Sammi, confidence in yourself," Mr. Carmalinghi said and patted me on the back. "Isn't that what I'm always telling you?"

"Uh-huh." I tucked a copy of that day's *New York Times* under one arm, scanned the mess we had made with Trivial Pursuit, and rose to leave. "Well, thanks for everything. I'll see you on the set."

"And I'll be rooting for you all the way. And

don't let that Dave Handlin get to you. Just try not to think about him." I turned around, my mouth half open. He winked at me.

"Um," I responded numbly, and I heard him laugh as I strode out the door. *Try not to think about Dave*—ha! That would be like trying to ignore a huge pink elephant in the middle of Main Street. At that minute he was probably being told the same thing by his adviser about me. The way they saw it, we were contenders in a big contest, not two high-school students dating.

What would happen to our relationship after "The Brain Game"? I wondered. If he won, I would feel jealous. And if I won? Would he be jealous of me, too? So jealous he wouldn't want to see me anymore? I knew what Derek would do in Dave's place. He would break up with me altogether.

But Derek and I were different. He never really understood me or why I wanted to be the best at everything I did. I guess I hadn't understood him too well, either. But with Dave, I always had a sense that our minds worked the same way. He could sympathize with my need to excel because he was the same way.

Then why was it I wasn't feeling confident that everything would work out as I got into my parents' car and drove home? Why was it that all I could think about were his arms around me, his lips on mine—instead of the game and winning?

96

And that wasn't all, either. I was also thinking about Dave not having money the way I did. It was so much more crucial for him to win. To me, it was just a contest. To him, it could mean his future.

As I drove up my driveway, I saw Dave's car standing at the end of it. We'd made plans to go have a hamburger together, and he'd obviously shown up a little early. He walked toward me as he saw me drive up. I stopped the car next to his and rolled down the window to receive his kiss. His lips tasted salty and warm against mine.

"Hi," he said between kisses. "Have you been studying?"

"Mr. Carmalinghi's been quizzing me," I replied, still leaning out the window. "And you?"

"Doing a little trivia research. I guess we're now ready for the big battle."

I parked the car in the garage and ran back and jumped into Dave's car. We drove down to Cleo's and got burgers, which we took out to a small lake to eat. The sun was streaking the water with yellow bands of light. A few ducks sat on the muddy bank, and the gentle singing of the crickets offered the only sounds.

"You know, Sammi, I don't think I've ever felt so peaceful in my whole life," Dave said.

I surveyed him carefully, his strong, firm profile, his cool gray eyes, the easy set of his shoulders. "It is peaceful," I agreed lovingly.

"You know," he confessed, "my family is a noisy bunch. Living with a mob like that, there's nowhere to escape. I always felt a little smothered by it. But now, I feel free because I'm special. 'The Brain Game' has given me that. I already feel victorious."

"Oh, yeah?" I swallowed a bite of hamburger, wondering what he meant by that. Did he think he was going to beat me, or did he just feel good because he was the only member of his team left?

Turning gently to me, Dave asked, "Don't you feel like you just have to win?"

"Well, sure, but—"

"That's how it is for me. It would mean a lot to my family and, of course, to me. Not only for the money—though that would be great, too. But to be the best at something. To be one-of-a-kind."

"I think I know what you mean." For him, it was all-important. For me, it was a fun contest. I knew, observing the determination on his face, that he couldn't let victory slip away from him as easily as I could.

"Let's walk," Dave suggested. We strolled around the lake leisurely, hand in hand, throwing bits of leftover hamburger bun to the ducks. Dave and I wrapped our arms around each other. I had a sudden, panicky wish that this moment would last forever, that we could forget "The Brain Game" and just be happy.

The remainder of the evening passed in a pleasant blur. As we walked back to the car, I felt as though I were aglow. I was really crazy about Dave. Later, after he drove me to my house, he kissed me. It was wonderful. But then, Derek had kissed me just that wonderfully before we broke up. I remembered the panic I'd felt then, wondering if we really were losing each other. *But Dave isn't Derek*, I reminded myself.

Dave took both my hands in his and grasped them firmly, staring into my eyes. His gaze seemed to search mine so intently that I shivered in response. "Good night, and good luck tomorrow," he whispered, his lips brushing mine one last time before we parted.

Chapter Eleven

The studio was a madhouse the next day. A local television crew was outside the building, waiting for us to arrive. *Great*, I thought, *now they can show me shaking on the ten o'clock news.* They were making a big deal about this particular edition of "The Brain Game" because we were local Springfield students, not kids from other towns.

One of my favorite newscasters, Will Nyland, was there, and he wanted to interview me. At any other time, I would've been absolutely ecstatic. But because of my present state, seeing him only succeeded in making me even more nervous.

Will strode toward me across the parking lot. "Hi, Will," I greeted him, thinking that it must be nice to be recognized instantly.

"Hi. You're Sammi Edwards, right?"

I giggled at the idea of this celebrity recognizing me. "Yes, I'm the Wembley team."

"Congratulations on being in the play-off. How do you feel?"

"Nervous, but full of fire."

Will waved to his cameraman. "Hey, come over here, will you?" Trailing equipment, he moved over to where we stood. "Now will you repeat what you just told me, Sammi?" Will thrust the mike under my nose and asked me the same question.

Then he asked, "Who are you competing against today?"

"Dave Handlin of Rushmore High." My voice nearly failed me on Dave's name. "And he's tough." *Also brilliant, gorgeous, and wonderful,* I thought.

"And here's Dave now," he said as Dave stepped out of his car. "Can we have a word with you, Dave, for local station WIXP?"

"Sure."

"We hear you're tough."

"I am." He said it with utmost confidence and winked at me. "It's going to be a hard game today."

"Congratulations, Dave, and good luck." The cameraman stopped shooting, and Will said, "We'll talk to you again after the game. Have a good one, both of you."

"Now do you feel important?" Dave asked, grinning at me.

"Yes. I hope I can make a habit of being in front of cameras," I said.

Dave held up a fist as though it were a microphone. "For Sammi Edwards of Wembley High, this is only the beginning."

I giggled. "From the modest 'Brain Game' to the glamorous heights of television newscasting, Sammi Edwards is on the rise to fame and fortune."

"Let's get you through high school first, then maybe college—"

"You think I'm a dreamer," I protested.

He pressed my hand in his. "I think you're great." His touch steadied me. I wondered if he was as nervous as I was. He didn't appear to be. In fact, he looked calmer than ever. Or maybe I was just getting used to seeing him nervous.

Once we were inside the TV station, it seemed as if it took forever for Lucinda to call us on the set. When she finally gave us the word, we jumped out of our seats like jackrabbits.

"Stiff upper lip," I said to Dave as I slipped ahead of him.

"No, Sammi, not too stiff. Not good for kissing." He leaned down and brushed his lips lightly over mine. "You look nice, by the way."

For the occasion, I had chosen a bright purple miniskirt with a pink overblouse and lots of jewelry—three brass bracelets and brass combs in my hair. I had put the jewelry on in the restroom after I left home.

"You look nice, too." Dave was dressed conservatively in a suit; his one concession to flamboyance was a red- and black-striped tie, which I tugged on playfully before we took our places.

"The group feels smaller, doesn't it?" Ty asked us, grinning widely.

"Too small," I replied, shivering.

"The only consolation is that it'll be over before you know it," Ty said.

"Just like the dentist," Dave said and laughed.

The audience filed in, and I saw my father glaring at me. Of course, it was because of the outfit. *Why can't Dad just allow me to be myself?* I wondered for the thousandth time.

When everyone was seated, Ty asked us a couple of warm-up questions and gave us an unnecessary run-down on the rules. Then he told a couple of jokes, just to calm us down. Finally he said, "One minute from show time, countdown . . ."

Ty flashed his television smile as the Vivaldi music wafted through the little room. Cameras whirled, and the announcer's voice opened the show. Then Ty followed: "Welcome tonight, folks, to the final play-off of 'The Brain Game.' We have the two survivors of this edition. Both our players are anxious to win the individual prize money. Tonight's game will decide only that winner because Wembley High has already won the team prize. Even if Dave Handlin wins this game, Wembley will still get the five-thousand-dollar-school prize." Then he related the rules quickly, and we introduced ourselves.

"Hi, I'm David Handlin, and I'm interested in history and beating Sammi Edwards." He flashed a smile my way, the crowd applauded wildly, and my face grew hot.

"I'm Sammi Edwards, and I want to go into newscasting, but first I want to win this game." Wembley whooped with excitement. I caught Melody's gaze, and she waved.

"We'll begin now with the first question," Ty said, consulting his cards. "What is the chemical symbol for sulfuric acid?"

Dave buzzed before I did. "H_2SO_4."

A simple question. I knew the answer, but not quickly enough. Chemistry wasn't my favorite subject. I looked up, meeting Dave's beaming face as Ty awarded him the first ten points. *There are more points to be made,* I told myself. But I also liked the way Dave looked when he was triumphant.

"Sammi or Dave, tell me two things that sulfuric acid is used for?"

I pressed my buzzer, but not before Dave. He

was really on top of things that day. "Making explosives and fertilizers," he said.

"Correct, David Handlin, twenty points for you." Ty motioned to the scoreboard, where the numbers clacked up next to my zero.

"Who was Thalia in Greek mythology?" Ty asked.

I buzzed, just beating Dave by a millisecond. "The muse of comedy," I replied.

"Correct answer, Sammi. Ten points for Wembley to twenty for Rushmore. OK, moving right along here, name the Greek hero whose journey home from the Trojan War was celebrated by Homer."

I buzzed before Dave again. "Odysseus."

"That is correct, Sammi! Twenty points now for both Wembley and Rushmore. Next, name the Roman hero whose journey home from the Trojan War was told by Virgil."

I didn't know the answer to that one, and Dave pressed his buzzer almost instantly. "Aeneas," he replied.

"Correct answer, David, bringing Rushmore up to a big thirty points to Wembley's twenty."

The Rushmore section applauded enthusiastically. "On with the show!" exclaimed Ty as he glanced down at his next question. "What was the name given the route that traders used in ancient times to travel from the west to China?"

I looked over and saw Dave going for his

buzzer. I knew the answer, but for that instant, warmth rippled over me just looking at him— until his buzzer alerted me to what was going on. I was daydreaming.

"The Silk Road," he replied jubilantly.

"Correct answer. Forty points now for Rushmore to Wembley's twenty!"

The crowd clapped wildly. A cold sweat broke out across my back, and rivulets of water trickled down between my shoulder blades. It was warm, made even warmer by the pressure of competing against the boy I loved. Feeling slightly dizzy, I looked away from Dave.

"President Eisenhower," Ty said, signed a bill creating a network for national transportation in the 1950s. What is the name of that network?"

I buzzed. "The interstate highway system."

"Correct answer, Sammi. Thirty points for your team to Rushmore's forty. OK, who led the mutiny on the *Bounty*, in the Nordhoff and Hall trilogy?"

I buzzed. "Fletcher Christian." *Mutiny on the Bounty* was a book I'd read in English that year.

"Correct, Sammi, bringing Wembley and Rushmore to a tie at forty points at the end of the first part of 'The Brain Game.' We'll take a moment here to get a look at our two competing schools and give our contestants a break."

The film came on, but neither Dave nor I watched it. He studied me, and I smiled. I saw him curling up the edge of his note pad between his thumb and forefinger, a nervous gesture I hadn't noticed before. Of course, I had nervous gestures, too. I had a terrible urge to bite my fingernails. But instead, I rubbed my sweaty palms on the front of my miniskirt.

Within minutes we were back on the air again. "Welcome back to the second part of 'The Brain Game.' As you can see by our scoreboard, our teams are tied. Here we go. Name the Florida Indian tribe that once staged an uprising against the U.S.?"

Dave hit his buzzer. "The Seminoles."

"Correct answer for Rushmore! That team now has fifty points to Wembley's forty. OK, name the Cherokee chief who provided his tribe with a written language."

I beat Dave to the buzzer. "Sequoyah."

"Sequoyah is the correct answer, Sammi. Our teams are now tied at fifty points each. The next question is a visual one." A screen behind Ty's head depicted the symbolic five rings of the Olympic games. "What do the five rings symbolize?" he asked.

With a concerted effort, I didn't look at Dave, just quickly hit my buzzer. "Five continents."

"Sixty points for Wembley. The first Olympic games on record took place in Olympia in 776

B.C. Tell us, for ten points apiece, when did the modern Olympic games start, and where were they first held?"

Both Dave and I buzzed almost simultaneously. "They began in 1896," he blurted out before I could open my mouth. "In Olympia."

"The first answer is correct, but the second answer is not. Sammi?" Ty turned his attention to me.

"Athens," I said.

"Correct, Athens was where the first modern Olympic games were held. OK, we now have seventy points for Wembley, sixty points for Rushmore. Now, in the novel *Treasure Island*, by Robert Louis Stevenson, who led the mutiny on the ship *Hispaniola*?"

I hit my buzzer before Dave. "Long John Silver," I announced.

"Correct answer, Sammi, giving your team ten more points, a big eighty points for Wembley to Rushmore's sixty."

I flashed Dave a big grin, but his return expression was one of concentration, and only the flicker of a smile showed at the corners of his mouth.

"English is not a romance language," Ty explained. "To what language group does English belong?"

Dave buzzed. "Germanic," he answered.

"Germanic, or Teutonic, is correct. Rushmore

now has a big seventy points to Wembley's eighty." Ty glanced down at his question cards. "What is *terra firma*?"

Latin, I thought, hesitating.

"Solid ground," Dave replied.

"Solid ground is correct. *Terra firma* is the Latin term," Ty explained. "Rushmore and Wembley are now tied at eighty points each as we end the second portion of our show. It's a tough fight here, with two evenly matched opponents. But we'll have a winner soon." Ty turned to Dave and me and said, "That one about the Olympics was a bit tricky, but you both did well."

"I've run across it playing Trivial Pursuit," Dave told him, his smile reaching out and touching me.

"Wow, this is hard!" I exclaimed.

"You're doing great. Keep it up, Sammi." Dave was encouraging me.

Just then Lucinda signaled that it was almost time to begin again. Dave and I sat up in our chairs and got ready for the next grueling round. "Welcome back to the third segment of our show," Ty began. "Tonight, we have Sammi Edwards and David Handlin battling it out for the individual prize money of five thousand dollars. Wembley High has already won the team prize of five thousand dollars. Now we'll begin with this question. In 1853 the U.S. acquired land from Mexico to build a southern transcontinental railroad. What was the name given to this purchase?"

For a moment I thought about the possibility of losing him if I won the game. Which was more important to me? I stared at him blankly, barely hearing the question. Then he buzzed. "The Gadsden Purchase."

"Ten more points for Rushmore, bringing that team up to a big ninety points and breaking the tie. Wembley is still at eighty. Here's our next question. What role did James Gadsden play in the purchase that bears his name?"

"He negotiated it," Dave replied.

Ty consulted Mr. Krupp. "Correct answer, Dave. Gadsden was U.S. ambassador to Mexico. Rushmore has a big one hundred points now to Wembley's eighty." Ty shuffled through his cards. "On April 9, 1865, a notable ceremony took place on the steps of a courthouse in Virginia. Which courthouse?"

Quickly I dropped my hand on my buzzer. "Appomattox."

"Correct answer, Sammi. Ninety points now for your team. For ten points, tell us what happened there?"

I lunged for the buzzer. "Lee surrendered to Grant. It was the end of the Civil War," I replied confidently.

"Another correct answer from Sammi Edwards of Wembley High, bringing that team's score up to one hundred—once again tying Rushmore.

"This certainly has been a close game so far!" Ty exclaimed. "In 1936 civil war broke out in Spain. Many young American men and women went over to join the struggle. What was the name of the brigade they joined?"

Dave buzzed quickly. "The International Brigade."

"Correct," said Ty. "The unit was made up of volunteers from all over the world. Now, who was the dictator they were fighting against?"

I hit my buzzer a split second before Dave hit his. "Francisco Franco," I said.

"Yes! Wembley and Rushmore are tied again, now at one hundred ten points apiece. I've never seen anything like this, folks!" Ty exclaimed. "One of our contestants has got to give."

I glanced over and clearly saw the determination on Dave's face. It was obvious how much this meant to him. That knowledge nagged at me, making me think of what might happen if he didn't win. Five thousand dollars would help a lot toward his college expenses. I had it easy. My parents would pay for the whole thing. Sometimes life didn't seem fair.

"OK, our last two questions, contestants. What nationality was Florence Nightingale?" Ty asked.

I buzzed. Dave's smile flashed across my

brain, and I faltered. I was of two minds, wanting to win myself but also wanting Dave to win. There, I'd finally admitted it. I wanted Dave to win!

I knew the correct answer. I'd done an oral report on Florence Nightingale for a class the previous year. "American," I said.

"I'm sorry, that's not right. Dave?"

"English," he said over the din of the crowd.

"That's one hundred twenty points for Rushmore to Wembley's one hundred ten. One more question. We'll either have a tie, or one of these fine contestants will become the winner of this edition. What is a chronometer?"

Well, there was no hope now. I didn't know the answer, anyway. Dave pressed his buzzer, a triumphant smile already on his face. "An instrument for measuring time precisely," he replied, triggering wild applause through the Rushmore section. I broke out in a cold sweat once more as the knowledge that I'd lost the game began to seep in. What's more, I'd done it on purpose.

"That's it!" cried Ty. "David Handlin has totaled up a big one hundred thirty points to make him the winner of the five-thousand-dollar individual prize money. Our opposing team, Wembley High School, is the winner of the team competition, with three games to Rushmore's two. Thank you, Wembley Giants and Rushmore Royals, for these exciting games. You did marvelously, and we wish you the best of luck in everything you do. Join us next time, folks, for another thrilling edition of 'The Brain Game'!" Ty waved to the audience, and the Vivaldi began.

I raised my head to look at Dave. He grinned at me, joy written all over his face. I knew he wasn't glad I'd lost, he was simply glad he'd won. How could I blame him for that? I'd wanted it for him, too, otherwise I would've played differently. I was glad Dave had won, but I also felt let down. My father was shaking his head and staring at me.

Melody climbed off the bleachers and came over to wrap me in a big hug. "I'm sorry," I muttered.

"It's OK, Sam. You did your best. A really great job, I'd say." She squeezed me affectionately. "Dave was just really on target today. You can't know everything."

"I try to." I peeked at Dave, who was surrounded by Rushmore students, everyone hugging and kissing him. I was gripped by momentary jealousy. "He deserved to win," I mumbled under my breath.

Melody frowned at me. "What did you say?"

"Oh, nothing." I waved it away with a flick of my wrist, watching him move toward the studio door with his crowd of admirers.

Suddenly my family was around me. "You were wonderful, Sammi," my mother said, planting a lipsticky kiss on my cheek.

"Yeah," agreed Katie.

"Thanks, Mom, Thanks, Katie." I embraced them both.

My father scrutinized me carefully. "Good show, Sammi. But why did you have to wear so much gaudy jewelry? I swear, you could pass for a rock singer."

"Thomas—" my mother said, chastising him.

"You should watch what she wears, Beth," he shook his head. "She was on television, you realize—"

"Dad, sorry to embarrass you," I began passionately. "I apologize for having my own style. But we can't all be carbon copies of *you*!"

I stormed away from them, dashing through the studio and pushing open the double doors to the parking lot. I was so angry at Dad. He should have realized that that wasn't the time to criticize me. Tears gathered in my eyes, but I wouldn't allow them to spill out. I didn't want anyone to think I was crying because I'd lost the game. I would cry later, in the privacy of my own room. I stood by the car, trembling with emotions I couldn't sort out. My father, Dave, the game, it was all too confusing. Finally Dave broke free of his admirers and came over to me.

"Congratulations, Dave." I managed a smile as he settled beside me, leaning against a Chevy van. "It couldn't have happened to a nicer person." That was a heartfelt statement if ever I'd uttered one.

"Thanks. You played a tough game, Sammi." He brushed the back of his hand along my cheek. His gentle touch made me feel a little better. "Would you like to grab a bite to eat a little later?"

"Sure."

"OK. Last week's show isn't going to be broadcast tonight, so we can go at seven."

"Fine." Loving warmth seeped through me, melting my urge to cry. I decided things weren't so bad after all. I still had Dave.

Just before Dave got to his car, a newsman approached him and started asking questions. I wished I was him, then. But before I could bemoan the fact, Will Nyland came over. "How does it feel to lose, Sammi Edwards?" he asked.

I shrugged and smiled. "It never feels good to lose, Will, but I've learned a lot from the experience," I said. I figured that was the kind of thing people wanted to hear on TV. It also wasn't too far from the truth.

Actually, when I saw myself on the six o'clock news, I looked pretty honest about the whole thing. Nobody would ever have guessed that I had lost "The Brain Game" on purpose.

Chapter Twelve

I came home and changed for my date with Dave without speaking to my father. So that he wouldn't make any more negative comments, I wore blue jeans with a conservative blouse and sneakers. I felt uncomfortable in the outfit, as if I were trying to be someone I wasn't.

Katie surveyed me coolly. "Ms. Conservative tonight. Are you going for a job interview?"

"Ha-ha. No, just trying to pass inspection. Losing 'The Brain Game' is about all the rejection I can stand for one day." I really did feel bad about losing, even though I'd done it on purpose. I couldn't figure out why. In fact, if I'd given the game my best shot, I think I would have felt fine. Well, I'd made my decision in the afternoon, and I'd have to live with it.

"Going somewhere with Dave?" Katie asked.

"Uh-huh." We sat down and caught the tail

end of the news featuring Dave and me. We were still planted in front of the TV when he arrived.

As I left the house, Dad said, "You look nice, Sammi."

"Thanks" was all I said. Although I was so annoyed with him, I don't know why I said a single word to him.

I was definitely being mean and stubborn, and I hate it when I get like that. Mom says my father and I are similar in that way. We don't budge when we're trying to make a point.

"I'm really excited for you, Dave," I said once we were outside. "I don't know if that came across this afternoon."

"Thanks. I could tell. You did so well on the game. The only thing I didn't like about winning was having you lose."

"Look who I lost to." I grinned. "That makes a difference. Did you think I'd be angry at you?"

He shrugged. "I guess not. I know I wouldn't have been mad at you if you'd won."

"That's nice to hear," I said softly. "Are you going to do something wild with a little bit of your prize money?"

"I think I'll use it all on something frivolous, like college, thank you."

We laughed. I liked Dave's sense of humor. He made me forget about losing the game.

"Everybody's meeting at Sunday's for dinner," Dave said.

"To celebrate your victory," I added.

"And your good sportsmanship," he said, reaching for my hand. His touch sent a tingle through me. Why did he affect me that way? With Dave around, I was likely never to have a clear thought again.

We drove to Sunday's. It was a pizza place, but much nicer than the Pizza Hut. As soon as we stepped inside, people came over to greet us. It seemed as though most of the students from both Wembley and Rushmore were there. A lot of people wanted to talk to Dave.

"Hey, Dave. Fine game."

"We're ecstatic—congratulations."

"Good show, Sam."

"You mean you two are still speaking?"

"Sammi gets the Good Sportsmanship Award," Dave said. We finally managed to get two Cokes and slip through the crowd. Dave chose an intimate table for two in the back. There was a tiny candle on the table.

"Well, if this isn't the most romantic pizza place you've ever been to, then I'll bet I'm the most romantic guy you've ever been with," Dave said, challenging me and leaning over to kiss me briefly on the lips. "What kind of pizza would you like?"

"One with everything on it."

Candlelight flickered across his features,

outlining his cheekbones. "Your wish is my command," he whispered.

I shivered. "You have a strange effect on me, Dave. Are you sure you're not some Martian with power over Earthlings?"

He nearly choked on his Coke. "As far as I know," he said, "I'm just a plain old American boy."

"Then I can relax," I said, toasting him, our fingertips grazing as our glasses met. "Congratulations. Here's to you and your success. May you be great at whatever you decide to do."

"Thank you." He appraised me with a hint of a smile at the corner of his mouth. "And may you always be such a good sport."

That comment made me feel a little guilty. I'd never thought of myself as a good sport, especially under the present circumstances. Still, I was glad Dave had won. It was great to see him so jubilant and watch everyone congratulating him. And I guessed it was fine for him to think of me as a good sport, even though it wasn't exactly true.

Our pizza arrived, and Dave plowed right in. I stared at my slice for a few minutes. I didn't seem to have much of an appetite. I'd heard that all kinds of strange things happen to you when you're first falling in love.

"You're not eating much," Dave noted. "Is my success ruining your appetite?"

"You wish," I said, teasing him. He blew me a kiss across the table, and I blushed. "I'm crazy about you, but I'm not going to starve because of it."

"That's good."

There was a moment when we stared at each other, and my insides began to melt. I couldn't wait until we were away from the crowd, alone, where we could put our arms around each other and kiss. It was all I could think of lately.

"Hey, big winner," a voice called out from a table near us. "How about coming over here and signing an autograph or two?"

Dave and I giggled. "I can't believe someone wants my autograph," Dave said. "Don't go anywhere, I'll be right back."

"I'm staying right here," I said with a smile.

Dave went over to his fans, and Melody took that chance to come over and talk to me. She sat down on the chair where Dave had been sitting. "You and Dave look happy," she commented. "You don't seem too bad for a loser."

"Gee, thanks."

She shook her head. "I want to know why in the world you missed the Florence Nightingale question," she said. "I seem to remember an oral report you did on her last semester."

"Well, uh, yes, I did." *Uh-oh.* Melody knew I knew that answer. I could tell her that I'd forgotten Florence was English, but then, I had never lied to her. I could trust her with my life. Also, I had this sudden need to confide in someone, so I said, "Look Mel, I don't know what you're going to think when I tell you this—but I answered wrong on purpose."

"You did what? How could you? Why?"

"Because—" I stopped short, and my blood seemed to turn to ice water.

I looked up, and I saw Dave staring down at me, his gray eyes smoldering. I hadn't seen him come back. He was rigid with anger and shock. I wished I could touch him or say something to make him soften, but even as we stared at each other, I knew it wouldn't work. I wished I could snatch those words out of the air and erase them. But they hung there like words in a cartoon balloon, too obvious to ignore. Suddenly I realized I had been wrong, wrong!

Melody's gaze shifted fearfully from one to the other of us. "Oh, dear," she said, getting up, "I'd better go find a seat." She hurried off.

"I heard you," Dave said tonelessly. He dug in his wallet and dropped some money on the table. "Here's the money for dinner. I'm leaving."

I stood up, wanting to reach out and touch him. But I didn't.

"Dave, I'm sorry," I said lamely.

"I don't want your apology," he snapped back.

"Don't you want to hear why I did it?" I demanded.

121

"I don't care why you did it." He turned to go.

"Look, I'm sorry. I didn't mean for it to turn out this way!"

Dave stormed out, and I charged after him into the parking lot. "Dave, please listen to me. I did this for you . . ."

He didn't reply. His face was set in fierce, angry lines. I watched helplessly as he got into his car and drove out of the parking lot.

I felt sick and out of control. I just wanted to crawl into a hole and die. I longed for Dave's voice, his touch. I wanted him like I'd never wanted anything or anyone before in my life. It was like when I was a little kid and I'd plead with my parents for some toy, saying, "I'll never ask for another thing again in my entire life."

Dave, I thought to myself, *you make me happy. I'll never ask for another thing in my whole life if I can have you back.*

I stood in the parking lot, remembering other, sweeter moments that had taken place in parking lots with Dave. Meeting him, for instance, and our first kiss. But now, I had to consider the possibility that I might not see him again.

As I trudged back inside Sunday's, everyone stared at me. They probably thought I was jealous because I hadn't won and that Dave and I were breaking up because of it. *Let them think that,* I considered glumly. *It's better than them knowing the truth.*

"Oh, I'm so sorry, Sam!" Melody cried when she saw me moving toward her. "I ruined everything."

"It's OK, Mel, don't kick yourself over it. How could we know Dave was standing there?" My eyes filled with tears. "Oh, I didn't want him ever to know. Me and my big mouth."

I couldn't stand being stared at by all those people any longer, so I pulled Melody outside. We got in her car and started to drive away.

"Why did you do it, Sam?" Melody confronted me softly, pulling the car out onto the state route. "I mean, to lose on purpose is really kind of crazy if you ask me."

"I know, but I was thinking about Dave not winning and how much more it meant to him than to me. I would do something like buy a car with the money, but Dave really needed it for college. It just seems unfair when it's so easy for me."

"Sure it does, in a way. But then, life isn't fair. It's unfair for you to sacrifice your possible victory for him. And in a sense, you *stole* his victory. How can he be proud of what he did when he didn't win it fairly?"

"Well, I didn't mean to do that," I returned. "I thought I was doing him a big favor. Doesn't he see that? But he won't listen to me. I can't even tell him I'm sorry." The road blurred in front of me as tears gathered in my eyes.

"Would you be happy if someone let you win?"

"I don't know. Oh, Mel," I said, sighing, "I should've thought about how he would feel before I answered that question, but there wasn't time. What am I going to do?"

"First, I'll take you home. But I think you need to talk to him," Melody suggested. At my house she patted my hand as I slid out of the car. "I'll be home if you need me."

"Thanks." I went in to see if it was OK to go out again. I looked up Dave's address. Then I got in our car and drove over to his house.

Dave's house was a white cape in need of paint. The lawn was neatly trimmed with a pretty flowerbed. Two little girls were playing out front, catching fireflies. They were about ten years old and very blond. I walked up the drive, took a deep breath, and knocked at the door. A tall woman answered. She had the same chestnut hair as Dave, worn short and curly. She smiled as if she knew me. "Hi, I'm Sammi Edwards, Dave's friend from 'The Brain Game,'" I said, introducing myself anyway.

"Hello, Sammi. I've seen you on TV," she said and laughed. Her smile made me feel immediately accepted. *Oh, good,* I thought. *She hasn't heard anything bad about me yet.* "Dave isn't home yet, but you're welcome to come in and wait for him," she offered. "I'm Alice Handlin,

124

Dave's mother. I don't know how we haven't met before."

"I don't know, either. But I'm happy to meet you now," I said.

I followed Mrs. Handlin inside. The house was cheerful and cool, with lots of potted plants. I could tell this was a house in which people felt comfortable. Mrs. Handlin poured me a Coke, then asked if I wanted to keep her company while she sewed.

"What're you making?" I inquired.

"A dress for one of the girls. You must have seen Dave's twin sisters as you came in."

"Sure. They're really cute."

"Do you sew?"

"No. My sister does, though."

I heard the front door slam shut and then Dave's footsteps. "Here's Dave, now." Mrs. Handlin rose to greet him, and I followed sheepishly, not knowing what to expect.

One look at him was enough to let me know he hadn't cooled down. "What are you doing here?" he demanded gruffly.

His mother, realizing something was wrong, glanced at both of us, then announced that she would be in her room sewing if we needed her for anything.

"Dave, I need to talk to you," I said hoarsely, after his mother had left.

Dave wouldn't look at me. He wandered over to the window. "There's nothing more to say."

"Please let me explain. I did it for you. So you could go to college without having to work so hard, and have the same chance as I do. I know it was crazy now, but this afternoon . . ."

He whirled around to face me. "How do you know I wouldn't have won, anyway? Did you think I wasn't good enough? Why wouldn't you play fair? You cheated, Sammi."

"I know. I mean, I'm sorry, really I am." I was stammering, fear and intense emotions welling up in my throat. I was sorrier than I'd ever been in my whole life. "It was a terrible mistake. I didn't mean for it to turn out like this. I thought everything would be better."

"Everything could have been just great if you hadn't felt the uncontrollable urge to cheat, Sammi," Dave said stonily.

"Look, I'm trying to tell you I'm sorry. I'd like to make it up to you somehow."

"There is no way to make it up to me," he said angrily. "I thought you were someone I could trust."

"I am."

"It's hard for me to believe that now. Go home, Sammi," he said. "I don't want to hear any more."

"Just 'go home'—is that all you can say? I wanted the best for you. . . ." Then I turned and ran from the house before I burst into tears. I didn't want Dave to see me blubbering away like an idiot. I wished I could make him understand. I'd given up something pretty valuable for him, didn't he realize that? Maybe I hadn't played fair, but I'd done what I'd done because it would be good for him. I was torn between anger and depression.

When I got home, Katie was sitting in the living room watching TV. I sat down next to her, thinking a program might take my mind off my troubles. But nothing ever slips by my sister. "Why've you been crying?" she wanted to know. "Because you lost?"

"Yeah, that's it," I said, snapping at her.

"Hey, sorry. Bite my head off. Next time remind me not to speak to you." She shook her head in disbelief.

I rarely get upset. But right then I was not my usual self. I stomped upstairs and locked myself in the bathroom. I ran a hot shower and let the water assault me until I was bright red. Then I went to my room and flopped down on my bed. I couldn't believe what had gone on in the last twenty-four hours. Truthfully, I didn't want to, either. All I had now were regrets, the major one being that I'd hurt Dave.

I heard Mom on her way up to my room and Katie's shrill cry, "I think Sammi wants to be by herself right now, Mom." I appreciated that. She knew I didn't feel like talking.

"I'll be here if you need me, Sammi," Mom called through the door.

I muttered thanks, knowing that she thought I was simply upset about losing the game. Little did she know what I was feeling. I was all broken up inside. I was a fool, a complete fool. I'd not only lost "The Brain Game," I'd lost Dave as well.

Chapter Thirteen

With all my troubles, I'd forgotten that it was my father's birthday on Monday. Katie reminded me, and we decided to go shopping Monday morning. We had enough money to buy him a plain blue oxford-cloth shirt. That's my father for you. You can't buy him unusual shirts—or even shirts with stripes or plaids. He has to have solid colors.

At the mall a salesperson showed us a flowered Hawaiian shirt. "Not for our Dad," Katie explained. "He likes his shirts the same as his hamburgers, plain, with nothing on them."

After we picked the perfect shirt for Dad, Katie treated me to lunch. I was so depressed; I had merely trudged through the stores by Katie's side like a zombie.

"Food is what you need," Katie said. "You're starving yourself for love, and you don't even know if Dave appreciates it. I wish I knew what happened between you two." She eyed me with interest.

But I wouldn't tell her. I was too ashamed of myself by now. "Dave couldn't care less if I starved myself. I could just wilt away," I said, feeling sorry for myself.

"Dave likes you a lot, Sam. Boy, you must've had some argument," Katie surmised.

"We did. We're not speaking, and it looks like the end."

"That was an awfully short relationship you had."

"Hmmm." I didn't want to discuss it. I was angry at Dave, not just for his lack of understanding, but for spoiling what we had together. I would have been better off beating him at "The Brain Game" and buying a car. At least then we would have stayed together. But that was in the past. Now was a different story.

That night we took Dad out to dinner. I planned to wear a nearly new polka dot dress. Even Katie thought it was great. She chose a slim-fitting purple dress because purple was Dad's favorite color. "Daddy's little girl," I said, teasing her.

"Oh, shut up. If you wouldn't insist on being such a noncomformist, you'd get along fine with him, too."

As it turned out, Dad was in a bad mood.

Something had happened at the office. I purposely hadn't worn any outlandish jewelry because I knew how mad he could get about that. But the polka dots were enough.

"Sammi," he started out quietly, "it's my birthday. I don't want to have spots before my eyes all evening. That is the most horrible dress I've ever seen."

"It's a great dress, Dad. It's an heirloom," I protested, smoothing the pleated skirt.

"It looks as if you found it in an old trunk somewhere. I wish you'd wear something new, please, tonight." He turned to Katie. "Now your sister is dressed very elegantly."

"But I'm not Katie, don't you see, Dad? I'm Sammi, and I'm different!" My voice was raised, and I felt a little out of control. "Don't you ever look at me as just me, without comparing? Maybe you just don't like me!"

"Sammi, please," Mom pleaded. But I was already on a roller coaster ride and couldn't stop myself.

"No, I'm tired of being criticized. Most of my friends like how I dress. I'm not a carbon copy of other people. I like interesting old clothes. You understand, Mom."

"Yes, but—"

I cut Mom off again. "Dad just has a thing about my taste," I said hotly. "Talk about fashion snobbery."

"Are you calling me a snob, now?" Dad demanded, his temper flaring. "I will not put up with this, young lady. Especially after the kind of day I've had. Besides, it's *my* birthday. Change your clothes, and let's go out to dinner!" He was roaring mad.

Mom and Katie slinked around, trying to humor him while I changed into a boring gray dress I had stuffed in the back of my closet. My Aunt Gladys had given it to me as a gift once, and it was never my style. I hoped we didn't see anyone I knew at the restaurant.

Dinner was strained. I was on my best behavior, so much so that I didn't have anything to say. Mom and Katie made chatty conversation, just to ease the tension. Dad sat brooding over his food. I was so mad at him, I wished we weren't even related.

We got through the evening all right, but all I wanted to do was go home. What if Dave had had second thoughts and was trying to phone? What would I say to him? One part of me wanted to scream at him, and one part wanted to melt in his arms.

But when we got home, there wasn't a peep out of the phone. Later Mom came up to my room. "Can I talk to you, Sam?"

"Yeah, sure." I was lying on my bed, reading

Teen Town and trying to think about a good topic for my essay.

"I know losing 'The Brain Game' has been tough on you."

"It's not that, Mom."

"Then—Dave?" she questioned. I knew she didn't want to appear nosy about my love life.

"He's a large part of it, sure." I didn't want her to know he was almost entirely the cause of all my misery.

"And your problem with your father isn't helping," she added, inching her way into the subject.

"He's just icing on the cake." I shrugged as if it didn't matter, even though it did. I was too angry at him to admit how much he'd hurt me.

"Well, there's something about your father I've never told you. It might help explain why he's so difficult at times, especially about the way you dress."

"Are you trying to tell me there's an explanation for all this?"

"Maybe." She began as though she were telling me a bedtime story. "You see, your father is very proud. I don't think it's the way you dress so much as where you buy the clothes that bothers him. He feels he makes enough money for you to go out and buy clothes at nice shops, and it makes him feel bad that you don't take advantage of his money."

"But I'm saving him money," I protested. "What's he complaining about?"

"That's not the point. Your father can't understand why anyone would want to wear old clothes instead of new ones. Your father grew up in a very poor household, and to see you dressing this way reminds him of his childhood. Now that he's very successful, he wants all of us to be a reflection of his success. He can't understand what you're trying to achieve with your clothes."

"I'm surprised. I never thought life on the farm was so hard. It always sounded beautiful and simple," I reflected. I still wasn't ready to budge an inch for my father. This sounded suspiciously like one of my mother's ploys to put my father in a sympathetic light.

"Because that's the way he likes to remember it, I'm afraid. And maybe it's better that he does." She squeezed my shoulder. "Anyway, try to meet him halfway. Things might be easier."

"I knew there was a moral to all this," I grumbled.

She left smiling, but I was still furious. How could I meet Dad halfway when he wasn't willing to do the same? *Parents love to make kids feel guilty for everything,* I thought. Still, I knew I was guilty of being difficult. I helped spoil the dinner by being stubborn and angry and not trying to make conversation. Mom and Katie managed to say a few things that made it easier for us, why couldn't I?

I felt terrible. After all, Mom always managed to get around Dad one way or another because she loved him—and she tried. Well, maybe I could try a little harder to understand him. But I was too angry to really put my heart into it. I kept wanting Dad, and Dave, and everyone else, for that matter, to see things my way.

Chapter Fourteen

There was a cold war going on in our house between my father and me. We managed polite hellos at breakfast and dinner, but that was about the extent of our conversations. I just didn't know what to say to him, and I was still more than a little angry. Mom filled in all the empty spaces with lots of talk, and Katie offered anecdotes about her summer school class.

I ended up choosing Amelia Earhart as the heroine for my essay. She was so incredibly brave, and I wanted to relate to someone brave. I figured I would need to be tough to weather Dave's silence.

A few times I walked over to the phone, tempted to pick it up and dial his number. Then to keep myself from calling, I would pick up our family photo album and browse through it. There were pictures of Mom and her parents when she was little, her sisters and brothers. But there was only one studio portrait of my father, when he was in his teens, no other photos of him at all. Why? I wondered. Maybe they were in another album that I didn't remember.

I put the album aside and went up to call Melody. I had told her about the essay contest, and she had decided to enter, too.

"What about Martha Washington?" she asked. "Was she interesting?"

"Who knows?"

The next day, Saturday, Melody and I met at the library, which is one of my favorite places. When I'm there, it's as though the world doesn't exist. The library gave me a few hours rest from my problems. I found information on Earhart, then I looked at the articles about and by her on microfilm, which was fun.

Amelia Earhart was always different, even as a kid. She was an adventurer and spokesperson for women's rights as an adult. She believed that women should have worthwhile interests outside the home and that all women should do something to justify their existence. She set a new style for young womanhood.

Reading about her made me feel small for losing "The Brain Game" on purpose. As I took notes on her, I thought about how she wasn't afraid to win, to succeed. She didn't hold herself back for anyone—and in those days it was customary for women to take a second place. Her husband, George Putnam, wouldn't have wanted her to. Well, maybe doing my very best on this essay would make up for having thrown the game, at least in my own mind.

Dave had never wanted me to do anything but succeed, either. He had never expected me to lose, especially not for him, and I knew he would've been delighted if I'd won fair and square.

As Melody and I were walking home from the library, I told her that I knew I'd been wrong by throwing the game.

"You should've known you'd done the wrong thing, Sammi, when you couldn't tell anyone about it," Melody pointed out.

"That's true. I just wanted him to win more than me," I said. "I wish I hadn't been so impulsive." And I thought to myself, *I wish I could have a brain transplant that would turn me into a different person—someone Dave would like.*

"That's the gamble, I guess. If you don't have the guts to take chances in life, you miss great opportunities. But you also risk making wrong decisions by acting too fast. You know Dave might have won fairly, if not for you."

"I keep thinking about that, too," I said, feeling as heavy as a lead brick.

"Aw, come on." Melody patted my hand. "Maybe someday you'll speak to each other

again. Maybe you'll make up. Sometimes your
fantasies do come true."

"Right," I said glumly. "Don't I wish it."

When I got home, no one was there. I found a
note on the kitchen table saying that my parents
and Katie had gone down to the mall for ice-
cream sodas. I didn't feel like swimming, reading, or watching TV, so I decided to find the
missing photo album, the one I figured must
have all the pictures of my father as a kid.

I finally found two, tucked away at the top of a
bookshelf. One was filled with my parents'
wedding pictures, and another had shots of
Katie and me when we were growing up. Then
something slipped out of one of the albums. A
yellowed, faded photo of my father's parents
and my father as a little boy. He wore a funny,
uncertain smile on his face, and his hair was
slicked down flat against his head. They were
all dressed up in what appeared to be their
Sunday best.

Just then I heard my family come in. "What
are you doing, Sammi?" Mom asked when she
saw me sitting on the floor with the albums.

"Looking at old pictures," I said, slipping the
photo of my father into my sweatshirt pocket.
"There aren't pictures of Dad's family in here."

My mother smiled sadly. "That's because most
of his family photos were lost in a fire. There are

so few remnants of his childhood left. Why don't you come in the kitchen and talk for a while?"

"OK." I picked up the albums and shoved them back in the bookcase.

Mom had made iced tea, and the whole family sat around the kitchen table and talked. It was sort of like old times, when we were younger and our lives weren't so separate from our parents'. I talked about my Amelia Earhart essay and the contest, which my father was very interested in. It was the first time we'd had a real conversation since his birthday.

As we were talking, I tried to match his face to that of the little boy with the uncertain smile on the old photo. Sure, there were resemblances, but my father was someone else now. But deep down inside, the little boy was still there. I knew that, because deep down in me was the little girl I used to be, and still was sometimes.

"What are you thinking about, Sammi?" Dad asked me when we were left alone in the kitchen.

"The contest and how I plan to win," I told him, not wanting to tell him my true thoughts.

"I have utmost confidence in you, my individualistic daughter." He grinned.

"Thanks, Dad." My anger toward him seemed to have disappeared. There wasn't any reason for it anymore. But I still had something I wanted to say to him. "Dad, about the other night—I wanted you to have a happy birthday. . . ."

"Oh, I know you did. But what about the card you and Katie gave me? 'Another year of being you is something to celebrate.' I wasn't sure if you meant that, Sammi."

"I did. I know it's hard to tell sometimes." I leaned over and gave him a good-night kiss. That's how it is between my father and me. We fight, then we make up. But no matter how mad we get at each other, he's always there for me.

When I went up to bed, I pulled out the photo of him and his parents and remembered what Mom had said about the fire. What a history went up with those flames, a history I knew my father would rather not talk about. Maybe it was just as well. What Dad wanted was his present and future, not the past. I put the photo in my bedside drawer and switched on my portable TV.

A rerun of an old romance was on. As I watched it, I thought about Dave. I wondered if I could ever tell him how I felt about him, how much I admired him for his pride and honesty. But maybe I would never have known those qualities if I hadn't lost "The Brain Game." So, in a way, throwing the game did have a sunny side. Well, that might be stretching it a little far.

141

Watching the movie, I started to cry. My heart ached as I lay in bed, wishing he would call. His silence went on and on. Maybe he was so proud that he'd never forgive me.

Chapter Fifteen

The next day, Sunday, I glanced over the contest rules again, and I noticed that the deadline for the essay was a week from Monday. It had to be sent across the country, so I had to allow four days for mailing. That meant I had to start work on Earhart right away.

I called Melody to tell her, but she wasn't home. Then I remembered that we had put all our library books in her pack, so mine were at her house. And she'd told me she was going on a picnic with her family on Sunday, so they wouldn't be back until late. To top it off, the library was closed.

Nothing was working out. I needed a few days to come up with a final draft. Now I wouldn't get my entry in on time, and all my dreams of winning this contest would fly out the window.

I thumbed through the encyclopedia and

jotted down some basic information. I consid
ered doing an essay on somebody else, but
wasn't enthusiastic. When I do a report, I have to
do it on something or somebody that I'm really
excited about; otherwise, it comes out mediocre
at best. And I didn't want to be mediocre.
wanted to give this my best shot. I had learned
all this after doing a biology report on mollusks
which I was not the least bit interested in. And
got a C for my efforts. As I contemplated my
dilemma, I ate a few cookies. I was stuck
Unless—

I remembered Dave talking once about a book
he had on notable women in history. He had a lo
of history books, probably even a few with infor
mation on Earhart. Maybe he could help. If he
wanted to, that is.

But I was also afraid that he would think I was
using Earhart as a way to talk with him. And in a
way, I was, of course. But what if he turned me
down again? I didn't think I could stand that
Well, I dialed Dave's number, and his mother
answered. "Who's calling, please?" she asked.

"Sammi Edwards," I stated.

"Hold on a moment," she said, sounding a lit
tle uncertain. "I'll go get him."

After a moment, he picked up the phone. "Hi
Sammi." His voice was even, controlled. I wished
it were softer.

"Hi. How're you doing?"

"Fine."

Why did he have to be fine? Couldn't he be suffering just a little bit, like I was? "Look, I called for a couple of reasons. One personal and one not personal."

"Which do I get to hear first?"

"Do you want to pick?"

"I pick personal."

"OK." I took a deep breath. "I want to tell you again that I realize I was wrong to do what I did on 'The Brain Game.' And I'm really sorry. I didn't give you a chance to win, or myself, either. I wish I could take back that answer I gave and make things right."

"You can't change what you did," he said. Did I detect a softening in his tone?

"I know, but I want you to realize that I did it for you. I thought it was the right thing to do."

"Look, let's just forget it, OK? We don't have to talk about it anymore," Dave said.

Forget it? Forget what? Forget that five glorious weeks we spent together before I blew it? Was that what he was saying? "I just want to straighten out this—situation. That's all." I was choking sobs back.

"You're forgiven. Now what was the non-personal reason you were calling?"

"Oh, that." I'd almost forgotten poor Amelia. "Well, I'm entering another contest, and I need some information on Amelia Earhart." I told him the story of the books, Mel being gone, and the closed library.

"I might have something here." I closed my eyes and wished that he would invite me over.

"Do you want to come take a look at them?" he asked.

"Sure. Is it all right?"

"Yes. Let me look through my books. When will you be here?"

"In ten minutes."

I found a clean pair of jeans and a T-shirt, brushed my hair quickly, asked my dad if I could use the car, then rushed outside. Maybe there was a chance for us yet. He sounded pretty uninterested in making up, but maybe once we saw each other . . .

When I arrived, Dave's sisters were playing in the sprinkler out front. He answered the door, his cool gray gaze appraising me carefully, as if looking for visible changes. It had been over a week since we'd seen each other, and I felt strange and uncomfortable. It didn't help that his sisters giggled and whispered loudly about my being Dave's girlfriend.

"Come on in," he said without smiling. He led me to the living room and showed me two books he'd already selected about Earhart.

"This one features other interesting women as

146

well, and this one's a biography," he explained as I picked them up.

"Thank you so much." I held one of the books, unsure what to do next.

"Sit down." He motioned to a chair.

"Are you still angry, Dave?" I asked softly.

"No," he said. "I was very disappointed, though. I really like you, Sammi, but you didn't respect my feelings. Now I understand why you did it, and it was all very noble, but not necessary." He leaned down and stroked my hair away from my face. His touch sent a shiver up my spine. "I could've beaten you any day, hands down."

I grinned. Finally he was sounding like the Dave I knew and loved. "Oh, yeah?" I challenged. "I'm not so sure."

"Maybe we'll get a chance to try it again, but next time you have to play fair."

"You know I will."

"Thanks." Then he looked at me seriously. "You don't have to feel sorry for me, Sammi. I may not have as many advantages as you do financially, but I can make my own way. And I do. I have a good family, and I'm ambitious. I'm proud, too."

"I know that. And I don't feel sorry for you at all." I reached out and rumpled his hair lovingly. "After all, you've got me."

He smirked. "Now will you please tell me whether that's an asset or a liability?"

I narrowed my eyes. "I've got work to do, Dave," I told him, opening the biography of Amelia Earhart.

"Can I help you win?"

That was a way we could even the score! "Yes—you can read and critique my submission," I suggested. Dave settled down on the carpet, and I sat down next to him. We spread the books out in front of us.

We read for a while, a short while actually, before Dave put his arm around me and drew me to him. I had missed his arms around me so much that I just about melted at his touch. His lips met mine and sent tingles shooting through me. I never wanted to let him go. I hoped nothing would ever come between us again.

"Do you want to stay for dinner?" he whispered in my ear.

"Yes, I'd love to."

"Good. We're having homemade pizza."

I wrote a first draft of the Amelia Earhart essay over at Dave's house, then stayed for pizza with his family. I liked them. His parents and three sisters seemed to relate really well. They were very supportive, and they laughed a lot together.

After I helped Dave with the dishes, we watched some TV.

When it was time for me to go home, Dave

walked me out to the car. Leaning against a tree, he kissed me. The warm night wove its magic around us. He held me in a lingering caress. I wanted to stay that way until the last star faded from the sky. . . .

Finally Dave held me at arm's length, studying me intently. "I'm really glad you called me today, Sammi. I wondered if we'd ever be able to fix things between us."

"You know how I felt about you. Why didn't you call me?" I wanted to know.

"Because I was still too mad at you."

"I took a big chance by phoning you."

He nodded. "But everything is going to be OK. Don't you worry."

I sighed. "Right now," I said, squeezing him, "I don't have a worry in the world."

Chapter Sixteen

"May I have the envelope, please?" Dave asked me. We were headed from my mailbox to the swimming pool in the backyard. The mail had just arrived—with a letter from the essay contest. Dave stood in his red swimming trunks, looking lean and tanned on that hot summer day.

He slit the envelope open with his finger and read in a loud voice. " 'We are proud to inform you, Sammi Edwards, that you have won third place in our essay contest, for your essay about Amelia Earhart.' "

"You're teasing me, Dave," I said, taking the letter from him. It fluttered in the wind, and it took a moment to straighten it out so that I could read it. It was no joke. The letter continued. " 'Thank you very much for your submission. You will see it published in the October issue of *Teen Town*. A check for $250 will be in the mail to you within thirty days.' "

"Congratulations, Sammi. You're a winner!" Dave took me in his arms and kissed me.

"I'm so excited!" I said, hugging him hard.

"Let's celebrate tonight, OK? I'll take you to eat at Sunday's."

"Ah, you're sweet," I said, kissing the end of his nose.

We walked arm in arm back to the swimming pool. Dave jumped in and waited for me.

I landed with a splash just inches from him. He put his arms around me and kissed me, his lips tasting wet and cold, but warming quickly next to mine. "I love you, Sammi. Did you know that?" he asked gently. He pushed my hair behind my ears.

"I think I did," I told him between kisses. "And I've been thinking about my feelings for you."

"Have you come up with any conclusion?"

"Yes. I love you." I kissed his cheek. "I'm completely crazy about you."

His gray eyes lit up with mischief. I sensed he was up to something, but too late. He dunked me under the water. I flailed around, hearing his laughter as I popped up for air. Then he hooked his arms around my waist and pulled me up

151

against him. I pushed *him* under this time, and we both laughed.

Then we kissed again. And in his arms, I knew for certain that the most precious prize I could have won was Dave himself.

A LETTER TO THE READER

Dear Friend,

Ever since I created the series, SWEET VALLEY HIGH, I've been thinking about a love trilogy, a miniseries revolving around one very special girl, a character similar in some ways to Jessica Wakefield, but even more devastating—more beautiful, more charming, and much more devious.

Her name is Caitlin Ryan, and with her long black hair, her magnificent blue eyes and ivory complexion, she's the most popular girl at the exclusive boarding school she attends in Virginia. On the surface her life seems perfect. She has it all: great wealth, talent, intelligence, and the dazzle to charm every boy in the school. But deep inside there's a secret need that haunts her life.

Caitlin's mother died in childbirth, and her father abandoned her immediately after she was born. At least that's the lie she has been told by her enormously rich grandmother, the cold and powerful matriarch who has raised Caitlin and given her everything money can buy. But not love.

Caitlin dances from boy to boy, never staying long, often breaking hearts, yet she's so sparkling and delightful that everyone forgives her. No one can resist her.

No one that is, but Jed Michaels. He's the new boy in school—tall, wonderfully handsome, and very, very nice. And Caitlin means to have him.

But somehow the old tricks don't work; she can't

seem to manipulate him. Impossible! There has never been anyone that the beautiful and terrible Caitlin couldn't have. And now she wants Jed Michaels—no matter who gets hurt or what she has to do to get him.

So many of you follow my SWEET VALLEY HIGH series that I know you'll find it fascinating to read what happens when love comes into the life of this spoiled and selfish beauty—the indomitable Caitlin Ryan.

Thanks for being there, and keep reading,

Francine Pascal

A special preview of the exciting
opening chapter of the first book
in the fabulous new trilogy:

CAITLIN

BOOK ONE

LOVING

---

by Francine Pascal,
creator of the best-selling
SWEET VALLEY HIGH series

"That's not a bad idea, Tenny," Caitlin said as she reached for a book from her locker. "Actually, it's pretty good."

"You really like it?" Tenny Sears hung on every word the beautiful Caitlin Ryan said. It was the petite freshman's dream to be accepted into the elite group the tall, dark-haired junior led at Highgate Academy. She was ready to do anything to belong.

Caitlin looked around and noticed the group of five girls who had begun to walk their way, and she lowered her voice conspiratorially. "Let me think it over, and I'll get back to you later. Meanwhile let's just keep it between us, okay?"

"Absolutely." Tenny struggled to keep her excitement down to a whisper. The most important girl in the whole school liked her idea. "Cross my heart," she promised. "I won't breathe a word to anyone."

Tenny would have loved to continue the conversation, but at just that moment Caitlin remembered she'd left her gold pen in French class. Tenny was only too happy to race to fetch it.

The minute the younger girl was out of sight, Caitlin gathered the other girls around her.

"Hey, you guys, I just had a great idea for this year's benefit night. Want to hear it?"

Of course they wanted to hear what she had to say about the benefit, the profits of which would go to the scholarship fund for miners' children. Everyone was always interested in anything Caitlin Ryan had to say. She waited until all eyes were on her, then hesitated for an instant, increasing the dramatic impact of her words.

"How about a male beauty contest?"

"A what?" Morgan Conway exclaimed.

"A male beauty contest," Caitlin answered, completely unruffled. "With all the guys dressing up in crazy outfits. It'd be a sellout!"

Most of the girls looked at Caitlin as if she'd suddenly gone crazy, but Dorothy Raite, a sleek, blond newcomer to Highgate, stepped closer to Caitlin's locker. "I think it's a great idea!"

"Thanks, Dorothy," Caitlin said, smiling modestly.

"I don't know." Morgan was doubtful. "How are you going to get the guys to go along with this? I can't quite picture Roger Wake parading around on stage in a swimsuit."

"He'll be the first contestant to sign up when I get done talking to him." Caitlin's tone was slyly smug.

"And all the other guys?"

"They'll follow along." Caitlin placed the last of her books in her knapsack, zipped it shut, then gracefully slung it over her shoulder. "Everybody who's anybody in this school will just shrivel up and die if they can't be part of it. Believe me, I wouldn't let the student council down. After all, I've got my new presidency to live up to."

Morgan frowned. "I suppose." She took a chocolate bar out of her brown leather shoulder bag and began to unwrap it.

Just at that moment, Tenny came back, empty-handed and full of apologies. "Sorry, Caitlin, I asked all over, but nobody's seen it."

"That's okay. I think I left it in my room, anyway."

"Did you lose something?" Kim Verdi asked, but Caitlin dismissed the subject, saying it wasn't important.

For an instant Tenny was confused until Dorothy Raite asked her if she'd heard Caitlin's fabulous new idea for a male beauty contest. Then everything fell into place. Caitlin had sent her away in order to take credit for the idea.

It didn't even take three seconds for Tenny to make up her mind about what to do. "Sounds terrific," she said. Tenny Sears was determined to belong to this group, no matter what.

Dorothy leaned over and whispered to Caitlin. "Speaking of beauties, look who's walking over here."

Casually Caitlin glanced up at the approaching Highgate soccer star. Roger Wake's handsome face broke into a smile when he saw her. Caitlin knew he was interested in her, and up until then she'd offhandedly played with that interest—when she was in the mood.

"And look who's with him!" Dorothy's elbow nearly poked a hole in Caitlin's ribs. "Jed Michaels. Oh, my God, I've been absolutely dying to meet this guy."

Caitlin nodded, her eyes narrowing. She'd been anxious to meet Jed, too, but she didn't tell Dorothy that. Ever since his arrival as a transfer student at Highgate, Caitlin had been studying him, waiting for precisely the right moment to be introduced and to make an unforgettable impression on him. It seemed that the opportunity had just been handed to her.

"Hey, Caitlin. How're you doing?" Roger called out, completely ignoring the other girls in the group.

"Great, Roger. How about you?" Caitlin's smile couldn't have been wider. "Thought you'd be on the soccer field by now."

"I'm on my way. The coach pushed back practice half an hour today, anyway. Speaking of which, I don't remember seeing you at the last scrimmage." There was a hint of teasing in his voice.

Caitlin looked puzzled and touched her fingertips to her lips. "I was there, I'm sure—"

"We were late, Caitlin, remember?" Tenny spoke up eagerly. "I was with you at drama club, and it ran over."

"Now, how could I have forgotten? You see,

Roger"—Caitlin sent him a sly, laughing look—"we never let the team down. Jenny should know—she's one of your biggest fans."

"Tenny," the girl corrected meekly. But she was glowing from having been singled out for attention by Caitlin.

"Oh, right, Tenny. Sorry, but I'm really bad with names sometimes." Caitlin smiled at the girl with seeming sincerity, but her attention returned quickly to the two boys standing nearby.

"Caitlin," Dorothy burst in, "do you want to tell him—"

"Shhh," Caitlin put her finger to her lips. "Not yet. We haven't made all our plans."

"Tell me what?" Roger asked eagerly.

"Oh, just a little idea we have for the council fund-raiser, but it's too soon to talk about it."

"Come on." Roger was becoming intrigued. "You're not being fair, Caitlin."

She paused. "Well, since you're our star soccer player, I can tell you it's going to be the hottest happening at Highgate this fall."

"Oh, yeah? What, a party?"

"No."

"A concert?"

She shook her head, her black-lashed, blue eyes twinkling. "I'm not going to stand here and play Twenty Questions with you, Roger. But when we decide to make our plans public, you'll be the first to know. I promise."

"Guess I'll have to settle for that."

"Anyway, Roger, I promise not to let any of this other stuff interfere with my supporting the team from now on."

At her look, Roger seemed ready to melt into his Nikes.

Just at that moment Jed Michaels stepped forward. It was a casual move on his part, as though he were just leaning in a little more closely to hear the conversation. His gaze rested on Caitlin.

Although she'd deliberately given the impression of being impervious to Jed, Caitlin was acutely aware of every move he made. She'd studied him enough from a distance to know that she liked what she saw.

Six feet tall, with broad shoulders and a trim body used to exercise, Jed Michaels was the type of boy made for a girl like Caitlin. He had wavy, light brown hair, ruggedly even features, and an endearing, crooked smile. Dressed casually in a striped cotton shirt, tight cords, and western boots, Jed didn't look like the typical preppy Highgate student, and Caitlin had the feeling it was a deliberate choice. He looked like his own person.

Caitlin had been impressed before, but now that she saw him close at hand, she felt electrified. For that brief instant when his incredible green eyes had looked directly into hers, she'd felt a tingle go up her spine.

Suddenly realizing the need for an introduction, Roger put his hand on Jed's shoulder. "By the way, do you girls know Jed Michaels? He just transferred here from Montana. We've already got him signed up for the soccer team."

Immediately the girls called out a chorus of enthusiastic greetings, which Jed acknowledged with a friendly smile and a nod of his head. "Nice to meet you." Dorothy's call had been the loudest, and Jed's gaze went toward the pretty blonde.

Dorothy smiled at him warmly, and Jed grinned back. But before another word could be spoken, Caitlin riveted Jed with her most magnetic look.

"I've seen you in the halls, Jed, and hoped you'd been made welcome." The intense fire of her deep blue eyes emphasized her words.

He looked from Dorothy to Caitlin. "Sure have."

"And how do you like Highgate?" Caitlin pressed on quickly, keeping the attention on herself.

"So far, so good." His voice was deep and soft and just slightly tinged with a western drawl.

"I'm glad." The enticing smile never left Caitlin's lips. "What school did you transfer from?"

"A small one back in Montana. You wouldn't have heard of it."

"Way out in cattle country?"

His eyes glimmered. "You've been to Montana?"

"Once. Years ago with my grandmother. It's really beautiful. All those mountains . . ."

"Yeah. Our ranch borders the Rockies."

"Ranch, huh? I'll bet you ride, then."

"Before I could walk."

"Then you'll have to try the riding here—eastern style. It's really fantastic! We're known for our hunt country in this part of Virginia."

"I'd like to try it."

"Come out with me sometime, and I'll show you the trails. I ride almost every afternoon." Caitlin drew her fingers through her long, black hair, pulling it away from her face in a way she knew was becoming, yet which seemed terribly innocent.

"Sounds like something I'd enjoy,"—Jed said, smiling—"once I get settled in."

"We're not going to give him much time for riding," Roger interrupted. "Not until after soccer season, anyway. The coach already has him singled out as first-string forward."

"We're glad you're on the team," Caitlin said. "With Roger as captain, we're going to have a great season." Caitlin glanced at Roger, who seemed flattered by her praise. Then through slightly lowered lashes, she looked directly back at Jed. "But I know it will be even better now."

Jed only smiled. "Hope I can live up to that."

Roger turned to Jed. "We've got to go."

"Fine." Jed nodded.

Caitlin noticed Dorothy, who had been silent during Jed and Caitlin's conversation. She was now staring at Jed wistfully as he and Roger headed toward the door.

Caitlin quickly leaned over to whisper, "Dorothy, did you notice the way Roger was looking at you?"

Her attention instantly diverted, Dorothy looked away from Jed to look at Caitlin. "Me?" She sounded surprised.

"Yeah. He really seems interested."

"Oh, I don't think so." Despite her attraction to Jed, Dorothy seemed flattered. "He's hardly ever looked at me before."

"You were standing behind me and probably couldn't notice, but take my word for it."

Dorothy glanced at the star soccer player's retreating back. Her expression was doubtful, but for the moment she'd forgotten her pursuit of Jed, and Caitlin took that opportunity to focus her own attention on the new boy from Montana. She knew she only had a moment more to make that unforgettable impression on him before the two boys were gone. Quickly she walked forward. Her voice was light but loud enough to carry to the girls behind her.

"We were just going in your direction, anyway," she called. "Why don't we walk along just to show you what strong supporters of the team we are?"

Looking surprised, Roger said, "That's fine by us. Right, Jed?"

"Whatever you say."

Caitlin thought he sounded pleased by the attention. Quickly, before the other girls joined them, she stepped between the two boys. Roger immediately tried to pull her hand close to his side. She wanted to swat him off, but instead, gave his hand a squeeze, then let go. She was pleased when Diana fell in step beside Roger. Turning to Jed, Caitlin smiled and said, "There must be a thousand questions you still have about the school and the area. Have you been to Virginia before?"

"A few times. I've seen a little of the countryside."

"And you like it?"

As they walked out the door of the building, Jed turned his head so that he could look down into her upturned face and nodded. There was a bright twinkle in his eyes.

Caitlin took that twinkle as encouragement, and her own eyes grew brighter. "So much goes on around here at this time of year. Has anyone told you about the fall dance this weekend?"

"I think Matt Jenks did. I'm rooming with him."

"It'll be great—a real good band," Caitlin cooed. In the background she heard the sound of the others' voices, but they didn't matter. Jed Michaels was listening to *her*.

They walked together for only another minute, down the brick footpath that connected the classroom buildings to the rest of the elegant campus. Caitlin told him all she could about the upcoming dance, stopping short of asking him to be her date. She wasn't going to throw herself at him. She wouldn't have to, anyway. She knew it would be only a matter of time before he would be hers.

It didn't take them long to reach the turnoff for the soccer field. "I guess this is where I get off," she said lightly. "See you around."

"See you soon," he answered and left.

Caitlin smiled to herself. This handsome boy from Montana wasn't going to be an easy mark, but this was an adequate beginning. She wanted him—and what Caitlin wanted, Caitlin got.

"You going back to the dorm, Caitlin?" Morgan asked.

"Yeah, I've got a ton of reading to do for English lit." Caitlin spoke easily, but her thoughts were on the smile Jed Michaels had given her just before he'd left.

"Somerson really piled it on tonight, didn't she?" Gloria Parks muttered.

"Who cares about homework," Caitlin replied. "I want to hear what you guys think of Jed."

"Not bad at all." Tenny giggled.

"We ought to be asking *you*, Caitlin," Morgan added. "You got all his attention."

Caitlin brought her thoughts back to the present and laughed. "Did I? I hadn't even noticed," she said coyly.

"At least Roger's got some competition now," Jessica Stark, a usually quiet redhead, remarked. "He was really getting *unbearable*."

"There's probably a lot more to Roger than meets the eye," Dorothy said in his defense.

"I agree. Roger's not bad. And what do you expect," Caitlin added, "when all he hears is how he's the school star."

The girls started crossing the lawns from the grouping of Highgate classroom buildings toward the dorms. The magnificent grounds of the exclusive boarding school were spread out around them. The ivy-covered walls of the original school building had changed little in the two hundred years since it had been constructed as the manor house for a prosperous plantation. A sweeping carpet of lawn had replaced the tilled fields of the past; and the smaller buildings had been converted into dormitories and staff quarters. The horse stable had been expanded, and several structures had been added—classroom buildings, a gymnasium complete with an indoor pool, tennis and racketball courts—but the architecture of the new buildings blended in well with that of the old.

"Caitlin, isn't that your grandmother's car in the visitors' parking lot?" Morgan pointed toward the graveled parking area off the oak-shaded main drive. A sleek, silver Mercedes sports coupe was gleaming in the sunlight there.

"So it is." Caitlin frowned momentarily. "Wonder what she's doing here? I must have left something at the house last time I was home for the weekend."

"My dream car!" Gloria exclaimed, holding one hand up to adjust her glasses. "I've told Daddy he absolutely *must* buy me one for my sixteenth birthday."

"And what did he say?" Jessica asked.

Gloria made a face. "That I had to settle for his three-year-old Datsun or get a bicycle."

"Beats walking," Morgan said, reaching into her bag for another candy bar.

"But I'm dying to have a car like your grandmother's."

"It's not bad." Caitlin glanced up at the car. "She has the Bentley, too, but this is the car she uses when she wants to drive herself instead of being chauffeured."

"Think she'll let you bring it here for your senior year?"

Caitlin shrugged and mimicked her grandmother's cultured tones. " 'It's not wise to spoil one.' Besides, I've always preferred Jaguars."

Caitlin paused on the brick path, and the other girls stopped beside her. "You know, I really should go say hello to my grandmother. She's probably waiting for me." She turned quickly to the others. "We've got to have a meeting for this fundraiser. How about tonight—my room, at seven?"

"Sure."

"Great."

"Darn, I've got to study for an exam tomorrow," Jessica grumbled, "but let me know what you decide."

"Me, too," Kim commented. "I was on the courts all afternoon yesterday practicing for Sunday's tennis tournament and really got behind with my studying."

"Okay, we'll fill you guys in, but make sure you come to the next meeting. And I don't want any excuses. If you miss the meeting, you're out!" Caitlin stressed firmly. "I'll catch the rest of you later, then."

All the girls walked away except Dorothy, who lingered behind. Just then, a tall, elegantly dressed, silver-haired woman walked briskly down the stairs from the administrative office in the main school building. She moved directly toward the Mercedes, quickly opened the driver's door, and slid in behind the wheel.

Caitlin's arm shot up in greeting, but Regina Ryan

never glanced her way. Instead, she started the engine and immediately swung out of the parking area and down the curving drive.

For an instant Caitlin stopped in her tracks. Then with a wide, carefree smile, she turned back to Dorothy and laughed. "I just remembered. She called last night and said she was dropping off my allowance money but would be in a hurry and couldn't stay. My memory really *is* bad. I'll run over and pick it up now."

As Caitlin turned, Dorothy lightly grabbed Caitlin's elbow and spoke softly. "I know you're in a hurry, but can I talk to you for a second, Caitlin? Did you mean what you said about Roger? Was he really looking at me?"

"I told you he was," Caitlin said impatiently, anxious to get Dorothy out of the picture. "Would I lie to you?"

"Oh, no. It's just that when I went over to talk to him, he didn't seem that interested. He was more interested in listening to what you and Jed were saying."

"Roger's just nosy."

"Well, I wondered. You know, I haven't had any dates since I transferred—"

"Dorothy! You're worried about dates? Are you crazy?" Caitlin grinned broadly. "And as far as Roger goes, wait and see. Believe me." She gave a breezy wave. "I've got to go."

"Yeah, okay. And, thanks, Caitlin."

"Anytime."

Without a backward glance, Caitlin walked quickly to the administration office. The story about her allowance had been a fabrication. Regina Ryan had given Caitlin more than enough spending money when she'd been home two weeks earlier, but it would be all over campus in a minute if the girls thought there was anything marring Caitlin's seemingly perfect life.

Running up the steps and across the main marble-floored lobby that had once been the elegant entrance hall of the plantation house, she walked quickly into the dean's office and smiled warmly at Mrs. Forbes, the dean's secretary.

"Hi, Mrs. Forbes."

"Hello, Caitlin. Can I help you?"

"I came to pick up the message my grandmother just left."

"Message?" Mrs. Forbes frowned.

"Yes." Caitlin continued to look cheerful. "I just saw her leaving and figured she was in a hurry and left a message for me here."

"No, she just met on some school board business briefly with Dean Fleming."

"She didn't leave anything for me?"

"I can check with the part-time girl if you like."

"Thanks." Caitlin's smile had faded, but she waited as Mrs. Forbes stepped into a small room at the rear. She returned in a second, shaking her head. "Sorry, Caitlin."

Caitlin forced herself to smile. "No problem, Mrs. Forbes. It wasn't important, anyway. She'll probably be on the phone with me ten times tonight."

As Caitlin hurried from the main building and set out again toward the dorm, her beautiful face was grim. Why was she always trying to fool herself? She knew there was no chance her grandmother would call just to say hello. But nobody would ever know that: She would make certain of it. Not Mrs. Forbes, or any of the kids; not even her roommate, Ginny. Not anyone!

Like it so far? Want to read more? LOVING will be available in May 1985.* It will be on sale wherever Bantam paperbacks are sold. The other two books in the trilogy, LOVE DENIED and TRUE LOVE, will also be published in 1985.

---

*Outside the United States and Canada, books will be available approximately three months later. Check with your local bookseller for further details.

INTRODUCING

She's gorgeous, she's rich, she's charming, she's wild! And anything Caitlin wants, Caitlin gets, and right now Caitlin wants Jed Michaels. She'll stop at nothing to get him.

From Francine Pascal, creator of SWEET VALLEY HIGH, comes CAITLIN, the irresistibly dazzling star of an exciting new trilogy.

The first book is LOVING, and you're going to love it! LOVING goes on sale May 6, 1985; book two, CAITLIN: LOVE LOST will be available August 1985; and book three, CAITLIN: TRUE LOVE, will be available in November 1985. Find them wherever Bantam paperbacks are sold, or use the handy coupon below for ordering.

Price and availability subject to change without notice.

☐	24292	IT MUST BE MAGIC #26 Marian Woodruff	$2.25
☐	22681	TOO YOUNG FOR LOVE #27 Gailanne Maravel	$1.95
☐	23053	TRUSTING HEARTS #28 Jocelyn Saal	$1.95
☐	24312	NEVER LOVE A COWBOY #29 Jesse Dukore	$2.25
☐	24293	LITTLE WHITE LIES #30 Lois I. Fisher	$2.25
☐	23189	TOO CLOSE FOR COMFORT #31 Debra Spector	$1.95
☐	24837	DAY DREAMER #32 Janet Quin-Harkin	$2.25
☐	23283	DEAR AMANDA #33 Rosemary Vernon	$1.95
☐	23287	COUNTRY GIRL #34 Melinda Pollowitz	$1.95
☐	24336	FORBIDDEN LOVE #35 Marian Woodruff	$2.25
☐	24338	SUMMER DREAMS #36 Barbara Conklin	$2.25
☐	23340	PORTRAIT OF LOVE #37 Jeanette Noble	$1.95
☐	24331	RUNNING MATES #38 Jocelyn Saal	$2.25
☐	24340	FIRST LOVE #39 Debra Spector	$2.25
☐	24315	SECRETS #40 Anna Aaron	$2.25
☐	24838	THE TRUTH ABOUT ME AND BOBBY V. #41 Janetta Johns	$2.25
☐	23532	THE PERFECT MATCH #42 Marian Woodruff	$1.95
☐	23533	TENDER-LOVING-CARE #43 Anne Park	$1.95
☐	23534	LONG DISTANCE LOVE #44 Jesse Dukore	$1.95
☐	24341	DREAM PROM #45 Margaret Burman	$2.25
☐	23697	ON THIN ICE #46 Jocelyn Saal	$1.95
☐	23743	TE AMO MEANS I LOVE YOU #47 Deborah Kent	$1.95
☐	24688	SECRET ADMIRER #81 Debra Spector	$2.25
☐	24383	HEY, GOOD LOOKING #82 Jane Polcovar	$2.25

Prices and availability subject to change without notice.